GHOSTHUNTERS

Dark Tower

Titles in the Ghosthunters series

Haunted School

Poltergeist

Deadly Games

Possessed

Dancing with the Dead

Dark Tower

GHOSTHUNTERS

Dark Tower

Anthony Masters

ORCHARD BOOKS

This book is dedicated to the following students involved in the *STRETCH* programme run by Valerie Singleton in spring 1996. They all discovered the Dark Tower

Elizabeth Alexander, Elizabeth Bourne, Chloe Campling, Charlotte Cooke, Alexander Dobres, Ellen Duffy, Amir Feshareki, Shiva Feshareki, Emma Gould, Alex Hammond, Katie Holbeche, Maximilian Lau, Rhodri Lewis, Kirsty Lytton, Ben Maddox, Tamsin Mead, Joss Paddick, Melissa Paddick, James Randall-Coath, Jessica Rose, Tom Ross, Michael Rowden, Catherine Scott, Max Snapper, Alexa Tibber, Jonathan Tibber, Madeleine Tibber, Katherine Waller, Christopher Wright

With acknowledgements to the Painshill Park Trust who are returning to its original splendour Charles Hamilton's magnificent eighteenth-century landscape garden in Cobham, Surrey.

ORCHARD BOOKS
96 Leonard Street, London EC2A 4RH
Orchard Books Australia
14 Mars Road, Lane Cove, NSW 2066
ISBN 1 86039 817 0
First published as a paperback original in Great Britain1998
Text © Anthony Masters 1998
The right of Anthony Masters to be identified as the author
of this work has been asserted by him in accordance with the
Copyright, Designs and Patents Act, 1988.
A CIP catalogue record for this book is available
from the British Library.
Printed and bound in Great Britain

CHAPTER ONE

Jo stood gazing up at the Dark Tower, watching the big black birds gathering in a great cloud, their cawing increasing in volume. She had noticed them massing yesterday – and the day before – but everyone else hurried past without seeing anything unusual at all.

Fairfax Park was one of the few open spaces in the East London streets, but in late autumn it looked so grey and soot-stained that few people even noticed the five oak trees, the scummy-surfaced pond on which no self-respecting duck would ever swim, and the barren flowerbeds which were no longer planted out. The Dark Tower, an ivy-hung Victorian folly, loomed up from the centre of the park, its round windows like sightless eyes, the ivy rustling in even the slightest breeze.

Jo watched the birds fly through the glassless top window, a steady stream of rooks and crows, their black feathers dusty and gloomy-looking. They vanished inside, and all she could hear was a muted rustling, the odd caw and the occasional sound of flapping wings.

She shuddered. Jo had always been terrified of birds, ever since one had fluttered into her bedroom. The rook must have been attacked by a cat because its feathers were bloodied and torn, but why the wounded bird had flown through the open first-floor window of her father's small terraced house had always remained a mystery. She had never been able to forget the rook blundering about the room, knocking into a lampshade, overturning a pile of books, smashing a china shepherdess and ending up on the carpet, making frantic little scratching movements until death mercifully came.

Jo lived with her father who was a salesman and was often out of the house for long periods. Her mother had died when she was only two years old and she couldn't remember anything about her.

Jo had been alone when the bird had died on her carpet, and she had crept over to the rook, fascinated despite her revulsion, only to see its eyes were as bloodied as its feathers. Perhaps the cat had blinded the bird and that's why it had accidentally flown into the bedroom and blundered about so much.

Jo had picked up a wastepaper basket and emptied the contents on her bed, meaning to scoop up the dead rook and throw it out of the window, but when she tried to pick up the bundle of dark feathers she had been frightened by their softness and by the warmth of the body beneath.

Eventually, Bob Grant had returned to find his daughter huddled on the bed, weeping in terror, telling him that the rook's corpse was moving nearer and nearer to her, creeping over the bedroom carpet. He had briskly thrown it out of the window and then held her close. Jo had been inconsolable for a long time.

Now, as she watched the Dark Tower, as she heard, or thought she heard, the dreadful rustlings inside, Jo was horribly fascinated again. She had been surprised to find herself walking through the gate of the desolate little park, and approaching the door to the tower. Of course there was always the special association her family had with Fairfax Park – she had known about that for years – but why the birds? It was as if she were daring herself to get closer to them.

A single crow flew back out of the window, wheeling above the oak trees and then slowly circling down towards her. As Jo gazed up into the twilit frosty sky she thought the eyes of the crow were fixed on her own. Suddenly the bird stopped circling and dived.

Jo froze, waiting for its slashing beak. Then she saw that the crow held a scrap of material. Stepping back, Jo fell into the dusty hedge that grew thickly around the park railings, and as she lay amid the acrid foliage, the crow dropped the tiny piece of red knitting at her feet, flew up over the pinnacled roof of the tower and disappeared into the night sky.

CHAPTER TWO

'There's something wrong with Jo Grant,' Jenny told her twin brother at break. 'She looks as if she's been crying. Do you think someone's bullying her?'

Jo was a loner and the trouble was that loners often got bullied. Too often. In fact, anyone who was different usually attracted the attention of the school bullies. Apart from being a loner, Jo also looked different. Her jet black hair framed a pale face and a beaky nose. She was small for her age, thin and slight, with teeth that had originally stuck out and were now being held in place by wires so they would grow straighter.

David and Jenny had tried to be friendly towards Jo, but she seemed to shy away from them. Her reaction to other pupils had been much the same, and as a result she soon got the reputation of being 'stuck up'. Jo wasn't popular with her teachers either, and was often in trouble for being late or not concentrating or failing to do homework, but she rarely showed her feelings. Jo Grant seemed to live in a private world of her own.

But now it seemed she had snapped. She was standing in a corner of the playground staring at a damp brick wall, crying silently, her long black hair half concealing her face.

As Jenny ran towards Jo, with David rather reluctantly bringing up the rear, they saw that Barry Workman, big, burly and malicious, had also noticed Jo's distress and was heading for her like a hungry vulture.

'What's up with you then, cry baby?' Barry sneered when he came into range, his little dark eyes in his thick pasty face mocking. 'Teacher been after you? Got into trouble again? You should wake up, you should.'

Jo flinched away from Barry, huddling against the wall and still crying silently.

David, who didn't like bullies in general and Barry in particular, strode ahead of his sister. 'Push off!' he yelled. 'Leave her alone.'

Barry turned round grinning. He hated David, largely because they had once fought and he had lost badly, bawling his head off in a far more undignified way than Jo. Barry had not forgotten the humiliating experience. But now he was bigger and ready to take David Golding on again. He was stuck up too, he thought. Right smug little prat. He'd get him this time.

'What's it to you?'

Jenny gazed at David in alarm. He was rarely violent, but when he got angry he could be very aggressive, particularly with bullies like Barry Workman. Jo, meanwhile, had stopped crying and was watching as the two boys squared up to each other. Then the bell rang for afternoon school. Would that stop the combatants, wondered Jenny.

It didn't. Barry lashed out clumsily. David ducked and the blow missed him. There was a brief pause. Then to everyone's amazement Jo kicked Barry's left foot away from him and he fell heavily on to his back, lying on the ground like a huge stranded whale, blustering and outraged.

David and Jenny gazed at Jo incredulously, but she looked as surprised as they did. 'I read that in a book,' she gasped. 'I never thought it would work.'

'You've broken my ankle,' yelled Barry. 'I'll report you for that.'

'No you won't,' said David.

'The bell's gone,' Jenny pointed out.

Barry was no longer in a fighting mood. He staggered to his feet and began to limp dramatically towards the nearest door. 'I'm badly injured,' he said. 'And you're going to be in trouble, Jo Grant, you see if you're not.' He was beginning to snivel now and was soon lost to sight.

'What was the matter, Jo?' Jenny seized her opportunity. 'You been in trouble with the teachers again?'

Jo shook her head.

'Then what?'

Jo hesitated. 'I can't stand it any longer,' she eventually blurted out. 'The birds want me. The birds in the Dark Tower.'

The twins gazed at her blankly. Had Jo gone mad? What was she talking about?

'*Who* wants you?' demanded David.

'The birds in the tower,' Jo muttered, shame-faced, as if she had let something slip and knew she wouldn't be believed.

'*What?*'

Jenny stared at Jo, not knowing how to handle the situation. What was more, she knew they had to get back into class or they were all going to be in trouble. 'Can't we talk after school? Don't you go home our way?'

Jo nodded. 'I suppose you think I'm some kind of weirdo.'

'We'll find that out after school,' replied David abruptly.

'The Dark Tower,' he hissed to Jenny as the teacher wrote up the class homework on the board. 'Isn't that the folly in Fairfax Park?'

'I think so.'

'We've cycled past that place so many times but never really looked at it.'

'The tower's covered in ivy,' said Jenny. 'It blows in the wind in a creepy way.'

'So you *have* noticed?'

'Only the ivy.'

'Who's talking?' asked Mrs Brownlow as she whipped round from the board.

As Jo walked down the corridor she just managed to avoid a large boot with an equally large foot inside that stuck out from behind a locker. Moving quickly, she saw Barry sitting on a bench grinning.

'I'll get you next time.'

'There won't *be* a next time.'

'You think Golding's protecting you, don't you?' Barry asked scornfully.

'I don't need protection,' Jo replied. 'I can look after myself.'

'He's a right little prat. Thinks he's a ghost hunter.'

'What?' Jo wished immediately she hadn't looked so surprised.

'He says he's a ghost hunter. Reckons he found a ghost dog roaming about this school.'

'I haven't heard about that.'

'It was before you came. The Goldings think they know it all. But they're nothing. They're loonies. Like you.'

Jo looked at Barry with contempt. 'I like them,' she said. 'At least they're not pathetic bullies.' She walked away, leaving him fuming with rage.

'The door's open,' hissed Jo.

The twins leant their bikes against the rusty iron railings of Fairfax Park and gazed inside. Sure enough the door of the Dark Tower was half open.

'I've never seen it like that before,' muttered Jo.

'Neither have we,' said Jenny.

Jo was fumbling something out of her pocket. She passed the scrap of material to Jenny. 'I found this here,' she said. 'I think it's part of a baby's cardigan.'

Jenny gazed down at the scrap of knitting. 'It could be, I s'pose. But then it could be lots of other things too.' She passed it to David who merely shrugged. He kept gazing at the half-open door. Had someone broken in, or were the Council cleaning the tower up at last? Or was Jo winding them both up?

'I keep dreaming.'

'What about?'

'A baby crying in the tower.'

Jenny gazed at Jo curiously. 'You say you *keep* dreaming?'

'Every night. I'm afraid.'

'What of?'

'Going in. But at the same time I know I've *got* to go in. And I keep being drawn nearer and nearer.'

'How long have you been dreaming?'

Jo hesitated slightly. 'Oh – two or three nights,' she said over casually.

'And how did you get this?' Jenny held up the piece of knitting.

'A bird gave it to me. A crow.'

David burst out laughing and even Jenny was taken aback. She gave Jo an impatient glance and then wondered if there *was* something wrong with her. Like in the head.

But Jo was completely unabashed. 'This crow dropped it at my feet.'

'Then you started dreaming about babies locked in towers?' asked David.

Jo gazed at him blankly. 'That's right,' she replied rather doubtfully. She paused and then added, 'The park used to be part of my family's garden.'

David was now beginning to feel that Jo was a fantasy merchant and was using them to play out some game of her own. She could even be crazy and he wondered if Jenny was thinking the same.

Jenny, meanwhile, was wondering if the reason for Jo's isolation was these strange fancies. Or were they more than that? She looked warily around the dusty little park. She and David had avoided it until today; it was a place where vagrants came and had a bad reputation.

'A long time ago,' Jo went on.

'You sure?' David gazed at her challengingly.

'Ask my dad.'

'He's not here.'

Jo's lip trembled as if she thought David was going to make fun of her, and Jenny quickly intervened. 'Tell us some more.'

'The tower's a folly. Sir James Fairfax built it in the grounds of Fairfax Hall. He was one of my

16

ancestors.'

'But your name's Grant,' rapped out David, still deeply suspicious, despite the fact that Jenny was frowning at him.

'Fairfax was my grandmother's maiden name.'

'Go on,' encouraged Jenny, frightened that her brother was going to put Jo off and they would never hear the story.

'There's not much more to say. Sir James built the folly so he could watch birds and paint them. We've got a few of his pictures at home. They're mainly of rooks and crows. He also put up nesting boxes on the roof and fed the birds.'

'Is that *all* he did?' asked David. 'Didn't he have a job?'

'He had private money.'

'Lucky him.'

'He travelled all over the world, bird-watching and painting. But then came the tragedy.'

'What was that?' asked Jenny quietly.

'He caught a mild dose of typhoid, and although it didn't kill him he infected his family. His wife and baby son died.'

'How awful,' said Jenny. 'What happened to Sir James?'

'I think he went abroad again. I'm not sure.' Jo

was vague now.

'And you've been dreaming about a baby – and you keep being drawn to the tower.' Jenny kept her voice gentle, but even she was feeling uneasy now. She glanced across at David and saw that he was listening at last, although he still looked sceptical.

'I'm so frightened,' said Jo.

'Why don't you go home another way?' asked David practically. 'Then you won't feel this – this drawing feeling.'

'I can't.'

'You *can't*?' He stared at her incredulously. 'What do you mean?'

'I don't know. The Dark Tower really scares me but I feel compelled to come.' She paused and then hurried on as if she was both frightened and ashamed of what she was saying. 'A horrible thing happened last summer. This rook had been attacked and blinded by a cat, but somehow it still managed to fly through my bedroom window and then it died on the carpet. I was so feeble. I lay on the bed and I thought the dead rook was moving towards me. Anyway, eventually my dad got home and took it away.'

'Is there any more?' asked David gently, penitent

that he had been so horrible to her.

'When my dad had gone I noticed my bed was halfway across the room. I must have pushed it *towards* the rook. I'm scared of what I'm doing. Don't you see? I'm scared of my *own* actions.'

Jo began to cry and Jenny gave her a hug. 'You're not on your own. We'll help, won't we, Dave?'

'You bet,' he replied. But David was wondering what they *could* do. Did Jo need to see a doctor?

CHAPTER THREE

'It sounds like you're being *told* what to do,' said Jenny suddenly.

'What do you mean?' Jo gazed up at her fearfully, brushing her long black hair away, revealing a pale, tear-stained face.

'Maybe you're *meant* to go into the tower. We could go with you.'

'Why?' Jo looked terrified now and David tried to give his sister a warning look. He was sure she was making Jo worse.

'Have you told your parents?' he asked hurriedly.

'I've only got Dad. No – I couldn't.'

'Why not? Do you think he'd laugh at you?'

'No. He'd just think I was going potty again. I had a sort of breakdown when I was at my other school and I was off for a long time. I had to see a psychiatrist.'

'What about?'

'Birds and babies,' she replied miserably. 'I thought birds were going to attack me all the time. Fly down from the sky and jab me with their beaks.'

'And babies?'

'I kept hearing them crying.'

'So it's been going on for ages,' said David. 'Not just a few days.'

Jo nodded.

'And you've been walking past the Dark Tower all that time?'

'No. We used to live about half a mile away and I didn't have to go near it. But then Dad managed to get a more modern house and we moved here a few months ago. It's been getting worse ever since.'

'And now the door's open,' said Jenny softly. 'What're we going to do?' she asked David.

'I think we should go in there,' he said, suddenly feeling it might be a good thing for Jo to confront her problem. 'Take a look round.'

'No!' yelled Jo. 'I can't do that.'

'It could help.'

'How?'

'Prove there's nothing there at all. That you're just getting yourself in a state.'

21

'But it'll be dark,' pointed out Jenny. 'We won't be able to see a thing.'

'We could use our cycle lamps.'

'No need.' Jo's voice shook. 'I've got some candles. And a box of matches.'

Jenny stared at her in amazement. 'Do you mean – you were thinking of going in there alone?'

'No,' insisted Jo.

'Then what do you need the candles for?' demanded David. 'Why did you bring them?'

'I don't know. I picked them up this morning – and the matches.'

'Were you conscious of doing that?' asked Jenny slowly.

'Yes.'

'Were you afraid?'

'Yes, but I still made myself do it. I knew I had to, even if I didn't know why.'

'Yet you had no intention of going in the tower?' asked Jenny impatiently.

'I didn't want to.'

'It's almost as if you're being bullied into it.' David spoke slowly, thoughtfully. 'Like by Barry Workman.'

'There's a difference,' said Jo. 'I'm not afraid of Barry, but I'm dead scared of the tower and I don't know why.'

'Let's go inside. All of us.'

Jo hesitated, gazing ahead at the open door which was now growing shadowy and indistinct in the gathering twilight.

'All right,' she said. 'Let's do that.'

The night was cold; a frost was already settling on the foliage in the park and there was ice at the edges of the gloomy little pond. The wind was light but bitter, and its darting thrusts seemed to penetrate their thick winter sweaters.

Suddenly Jo came to a halt, gazing up at the Dark Tower rising above the oak trees, one round window on either side. The ivy clung thickly to the crumbling brickwork.

'Just look at them,' said Jo.

Once again the rooks and crows were hovering in a dense cloud that was just discernible in the pallid light of a crescent moon. Then, as they had so many times before, they began to flutter through the top window from which the ivy had been pulled aside.

'I'm not going in there,' said Jo, her panic rising.

But Jenny was determined. 'We can just take a look,' she said. 'Even if we pop in and pop out.'

'I wonder when those birds are going to pop out again?' asked David uneasily. 'You can hear them inside.'

They listened to the cawing sounds for a while and then Jenny grabbed Jo's arm. 'Come on. Let's get this over. It'll make you feel better.'

'Suppose the birds touch me. Brush me with their feathers?' Jo's voice rose and Jenny gripped her arm harder.

'They'll be far more frightened of you,' she said. 'Maybe once you've actually stood in the tower, then all the horrible dreams will go away. That's what you were really trying to tell yourself when you picked up the candles and matches, wasn't it?'

But Jo didn't look so sure.

They paused by the half-open door of the Dark Tower, but all they could see and smell was musty darkness. Jo was shaking now. Her fear was infectious and David and Jenny suddenly felt almost sick with apprehension. They kept looking up, hoping the birds would emerge from the broken window and fly away into the night, but all they could hear was the shut-in cawing.

'OK,' said Jenny, 'we'll light the candles now.' She took the box of matches from Jo and lit the candle David was holding in his gloved hands. Jo's hands were shaking but eventually they had three candles well alight.

'Right.' David's voice was brisk. 'We'll go in.'

He made no move forward. Neither did Jenny, and Jo even stepped back. There was a long silence.

'Right,' repeated David. 'We'll all go in now.' He began to walk jerkily towards the door, holding the candle aloft, and disappeared into the darkness.

The two girls followed slowly, shielding their candles against the cold draught as they crossed the threshold.

Once inside the tower, the heavy musty smell increased. By the light of their candles they could see a wrought-iron spiral staircase, covered in cobwebs, climbing up to a landing above, but the flickering light was not strong enough for them to see any higher.

The room they were standing in was bare and circular, its damp-looking walls also strewn with cobwebs. The floor was made of stone slabs, most of which were covered in light green moss and liberally sprinkled with bird droppings.

Raising her candle high above her, Jenny mounted the first step on the spiral staircase and then the second. David and Jo followed. Then Jenny gave a gasp of shock and dismay.

Rooks and crows were perching silently on the long rusty iron railing that ran round the landing. Not even a rustle of dry feathers could be heard, and the silence was much worse than the cawing and fluttering as beady eyes were fixed on the unwelcome visitors.

'They're roosting,' said David, trying to be reassuring. 'That's all they're doing.'

'They're watching,' pronounced Jo. 'That's what they're *really* doing.'

She edged past David but Jenny stood firmly in her way.

'They want me,' Jo muttered.

'No,' said Jenny. '*We* want you, Jo. We want to keep you safe.' She gazed up at the birds and felt their eyes on her, waiting for the next move.

CHAPTER FOUR

'Come back down, Jo,' said David fiercely. 'Right away,' he added sharply.

Jo looked surprised, as if she didn't quite know where she was. Then slowly and in some confusion she came down, followed by Jenny. As they passed him, David caught a glance from his sister. He knew exactly what she was thinking. Jo *was* being drawn. But by who? Or what? This wasn't fantasy: she was being victimised. An image of Barry Workman's leering features filtered into his mind, but David knew he would be much easier to deal with than these malignant-looking birds.

He looked up at the landing. The black birds were tightly packed on to the railings, completely motionless.

Then a creaking sound pierced the darkness and David shuddered. He was sure it was coming from the landing, but it was impossible to see. The noise was rhythmic, as if something was rocking to and fro. David had heard the sound before but he couldn't quite place it. Then he remembered. Of course, Mum had inherited a rocking chair from their long-dead grandmother. It must be a rocking chair. Holding his candle up high, David's eyes searched the darkness but he could still see nothing.

'Yes,' breathed David fearfully. 'Of course it is.'

'Of course it's what?' quavered Jo.

'A rocking chair.'

'But what would make it rock up there?'

'I expect the birds set it off.' Jenny immediately tried to be reasonable. 'One of those heavy rooks could have perched on its back.'

But the sound gave no sign of slowing up and, what was more, they could now hear something else. A new sound. A kind of clicking.

'Can you hear that clicking noise?' asked Jo.

'Yes,' said Jenny flatly. She wanted to go now. The musty smell of the birds, the shut-in feeling, despite the fact that the door was still open letting in the early evening light, the strange sounds – all were becoming oppressive and she was finding it hard to breathe.

'What can it be?'

'I don't know,' Jenny said.

Or did she? A dim memory stirred, once again of a grandmother, but this time on her father's side. Grandma Golding. Eighty-nine years old and a fierce old tyrant who lived with another old lady in a block of flats in North London. They were always at it. Clicking away.

'Knitting,' said Jenny, her panic increasing. 'I'm sure that's the sound of knitting needles.'

'Do you think the crows are having a bit of a knit-in?' asked David with feeble sarcasm.

Neither of the girls laughed, and feeling uncomfortable David climbed up another couple of steps of the staircase and held up his candle again. The birds hadn't moved a feather and were still sitting in their crowded row on the railings, claws gripping, eyes rigid. Above their threatening silence, the rocking chair creaked and the needles clicked.

'Have you ever heard that creaking and clicking, Jo? Even in a dream?' asked Jenny.

'No,' she replied. 'Only the baby crying.'

'That's something we haven't heard yet.' David sounded almost put out.

'Barry said you were ghost hunters,' said Jo. 'At least—'

'I can imagine what he told you,' Jenny said quietly. 'We've had some strange experiences, that's all.'

'Is this one of them?'

'I don't know,' replied Jenny.

'You think I'm just some kind of hysterical idiot, don't you?' Jo sounded bitter.

'No,' said David firmly. 'Something's going on here all right, and you're in the thick of it. But we don't know what yet.' He paused. 'You're not on your own, Jo. We won't desert you. We're going to see this through whatever happens.'

'Don't worry.' Jenny deliberately tried to sound confident. 'We're going to find out what's drawing you. Somehow.'

CHAPTER FIVE

Without warning, the sounds stopped and the ensuing silence was a relief.

'Let's go,' David said urgently, wondering if the noise would start up again, but Jo paused.

'I want to get it over with,' she muttered.

'Get *what* over?' asked David angrily.

Jo didn't reply, but neither did she make any kind of move towards the half-open door that was still letting in a murky twilight.

What if it closes, wondered Jenny. What if we're trapped in this awful place and can't get out, can never ever get out? The candles were burning down to stumps now and she knew they didn't have much time.

'Come *on*!' yelled David.

'I *can't* go.'

'You've got to.' David was sweating despite the intense cold inside the folly.

'You've *got* to leave,' hissed Jenny.

'I've been brought here. I can't leave now. If I do, it'll all happen again. Next time I might have to come on my own. I'm needed. I've *got* to stay!'

Then the rustling began, and when Jenny looked up she saw them fluttering down, a dark host of birds with sharp beaks, angry eyes and talons.

'They're coming,' she yelled. 'Run!'

Jo was co-operating at last, hearing the beating of wings and hostile cawing. The rooks and crows were above them now, trying to hurl their feathery bodies at the door, to slam it shut. Anticipating this, David got his foot over the threshold, and as the birds descended he was able to hold the door open.

'Come on.' He wrenched at Jo's hand, but now she needed no encouragement. David felt a beak in his hair and howled with pain as the rook pecked at his scalp, drawing blood. His candle blew out and he let it fall to the ground. But his foot remained between the door and its post, still holding it open even when he was pecked again.

Jo slid through the narrow gap but Jenny, behind them, cried out in pain as the birds attacked, their feathery bodies submerging her until she was festooned in a dark mass.

Some of the birds were still flying at the door and David was finding it harder and harder to keep it open. When he turned to yell at Jenny he was horrified to see she was barely able to stand up. David didn't know what to do. He didn't dare leave his post, but he could see that although his sister's hands were continuously plucking at the birds, no sooner did she pull one off than another descended in a perfectly co-ordinated attack.

Then Jo was back in the doorway, shouting, commanding. 'Leave her. Leave Jenny alone!'

Suddenly the birds rose in a reluctant cloud and Jenny was able to run past David into the park outside. She collapsed on the frosty grass, sobbing and rolling, as if the birds were still attacking her.

David grabbed at his sister, sure that she was badly hurt, but when she rolled over yet again he could see that apart from some drying blood on her head and a torn shirt she had had an amazing escape. Or could it be that the birds had only been trying to frighten them away, to make Jenny an example of what might happen if they trespassed in the Dark Tower again.

'I thought they were either going to peck me to death or I was going to suffocate.' Jenny got shakily to her feet.

She turned her head and saw that Jo was gazing up at the sky. But as Jo looked up at the top window of the Dark Tower, the birds began to stream out into the night sky, vanishing into the frosty night. A solitary night owl hooted and Jo raised a hand as if in farewell.

'Why did they listen to Jo?' whispered Jenny, her eyes wide with terror.

'She was drawn here. She told us. Even when she was scared out of her mind, Jo was still edging towards the tower. The birds want her and they're not prepared to disobey her.'

'I don't know how to help her,' said Jenny. 'She's here for a purpose. But what?'

Jo was running back to them now, looking like a gawky waif again, losing all her aura of mystery as she gazed at Jenny and David.

'We think the birds need you,' Jenny said. 'You said so yourself. Do *you* know why?'

Jo looked at her blankly. 'I don't know what you're talking about.'

'It must be something to do with your family. Your ancestors.'

'What *could* it have to do with them?'

'You can command the birds,' exclaimed Jenny. 'You told them to leave me alone and they did.'

'I was just trying to help you.'

'But it worked. Why *did* they obey you?'

Jo simply looked afraid.

'*We're* not welcome here,' said Jenny forcefully.

'Do you think *I* am?' Jo demanded miserably.

'At least you didn't get attacked.'

'They didn't want any of us to leave.'

'They didn't want me and Jenny to take you away.' David joined in. 'They didn't want me and Jenny *at all*! The crow gave *you* the message – that scrap of wool or whatever it is. But we're not leaving you to be bullied by a flock of birds any more than we would leave you to be bullied by Barry Workman.'

Jo shuddered. 'I can't bear the thought of being with them – on my own. I don't even want to go back home. The birds might come for me there.'

'You have to tell your father,' said David.

'He won't believe me. He just thinks I'm the nervy type, like they do at school. Dad will send me back to the psychiatrist. He wouldn't accept what just happened: the birds and the rocking chair and the knitting needles. He'd be bound to think I need more treatment.'

'What about the history of the place? The fact that this used to be part of your family home. There *must* be some kind of connection,' pointed out Jenny.

'Dad would just think I was getting all worked up about an old story. Going crazy or something. Having another breakdown.' Jo paused. 'I mean – would *your* parents believe you if you told them what happened?'

David and Jenny thought carefully. Their parents ran a garden centre on a wharf that overlooked the Thames and had worked hard to make a success of the business. They loved them dearly, but Mum and Dad were always full of thumping good common sense. They certainly wouldn't believe in Dark Towers or bullying birds or the ghostly sounds of rocking chairs and knitting needles.

'You're right,' sighed David. He paused. 'But you can't move *in* with us. Even if you came over for a night, there would be the next and the next—'

'I can't be on my own. It's been building up. Now it's come to a head. The tower's ready.' She paused. 'Although I don't know what it's ready for.' Jo turned desperately to Jenny. 'Couldn't you come and stay? Just for tonight?'

'Of course I will.'

'Dad would like me to have a friend. I've never really had any.'

'What do you think?' Jenny turned to her brother who was looking worried.

'If you're going – I'm going too,' David replied.

CHAPTER SIX

'I'll phone Mum from the phone box over there,' volunteered Jenny.

Jo smiled gratefully and David felt protective. She certainly needed support, but for how long? He shivered, gazing up at the Dark Tower, now no more than a brooding shape in the freezing night. He had the odd and unsettling feeling that Jo was right; the tower had been waiting for a long time for all this to happen. There was an air of expectancy. Then he heard a faint cheeping sound and saw something hopping about on the grass in front of him.

David held up the only candle still left alight. It was just a stub, but it was burning strongly enough for them to see the scrawny, featherless and terrified-looking baby bird. 'It can't be more than a few days old.'

'There's the rookery,' said Jenny. 'Up in

that big oak.'

David gazed up to see the rooks nesting above, making only the occasional gentle cawing.

The baby rook was still hopping about in obvious distress and David knelt down beside it, unsure of what to do. 'It must have fallen out of the nest.'

He was about to pick the little bird up when Jenny hissed, 'Don't touch it. If the mother thinks a human being's picked up her baby she might not come back and it'll die.'

'OK.' He looked down at the baby rook which was staring beadily up at him. 'It's a bit late in the year for a fledgling like this, isn't it?'

They all stared at it in consternation.

'Let's go and make that call,' said David at last, but as they pushed their bikes out of Fairfax Park Jenny kept looking back. Then to her relief she saw a rook swoop down from the oak and gently gather up the fledgling in its beak.

'Look behind you,' she whispered. 'It's going to be OK.'

They watched the rook fly up into the oak tree again and disappear amongst its bare branches. Then a few other birds appeared, hovering over Jenny, Jo and David while the owl hooted several times.

For a moment, Jenny wondered if they had passed some test. Could the birds have been wondering if they could be trusted? If they were sensitive?

'Mum?'

Jenny had already planned what she was going to say. Although her parents had no idea that she and David were psychic, they had become involved in a number of adventures that had made their mother and father wary.

'Is it all right if David and I stay the night with a friend?' she asked too quickly.

'In the week?' Mrs Golding was suspicious.

'Er – yes.'

'Why?' Her mother sounded as if she had had a long hard day.

'She's a bit upset.'

'What about?'

'It's Jo. Do you remember I told you about her?'

'The one who's always late. And lives in a world of her own. What's wrong with her now?'

'She was bullied. By Barry Workman.'

'Didn't David have a fight with him? I hope he hasn't had another.'

Jenny realised she had approached the situation

the wrong way. She knew she would have to work harder now and groaned inwardly.

'No, of course not.'

'What's wrong with David then?'

'Nothing, Mum. He just wants to be supportive and keep Jo company. Help her out.'

'It needs two of you?'

'She's very upset.'

'And you're all sleeping in the same room?'

'No, of course not. I'm sleeping in with Jo – and David's on the sofa downstairs.' She wondered if there *was* a sofa downstairs, but there was no point in conveying any doubts to her mother now.

'I hope so. And her father's given permission for this sleep over?'

'He won't mind at all, Mum.'

'I *said* – has he given permission?'

Jenny didn't want to lie directly to her mother and tried another tack. 'He's very concerned about her. She's really worked up.'

'All right.' Mrs Golding suddenly relented. 'But you'd better not talk all night.'

'Of course not.'

'And go to school tired out.'

'Of course not,' Jenny repeated.

'You sound that way already.'

'I'm fine.' Jenny tried to sound bright.

'You'd better be.'

'We'll drop in for a change of clothes and a toothbrush.'

'That's good of you,' said Mrs Golding brusquely, but after a few more questions, her mother let Jenny ring off.

She returned to David and Jo, feeling drained.

'Did she give you a hard time?'

'You could say that.'

'But it was all right in the end?' David asked hopefully.

'Sort of.' Jenny knew she had done her best. Her brother would have ruined everything by getting impatient.

'I'm grateful,' said Jo, realising all the trouble she was causing.

'It's all right.' Jenny looked back at the park and flinched. There was movement in the branches of the oak tree. Were the rooks watching them with their angry little eyes? Were they going to follow?

David and Jo had seen them too.

'They're closing in,' said Jo in considerable agitation.

'You can't be sure of that,' said Jenny. 'You can't be sure of anything,' she added.

It's all instinct with Jo, thought David. Then he looked back at the haze of rooks and crows hovering high up in the night sky and knew that it was all instinct with the birds too.

'Is that you?' Mr Grant's voice was anxious as Jo let David and Jenny into the narrow hallway of the small house on the new estate.

When he came out of the sitting room, the twins noticed immediately how relieved he was to see her. He was small, like Jo, with the same glossy black hair but with heavier features.

'I've been so worried about you. Where have you been?'

'These are some friends of mine, Dad. David and Jenny Golding. They've been looking after me.'

'Friends?'

'I know it's a surprise but don't rub it in,' said Jo sarcastically. 'I've had a bit of trouble.'

'My brother rescued Jo from a school bully,' announced Jenny, giving David credit for his intervention. They had already worked out the story on the way home, determined there would be no mention of the Dark Tower and its inhabitants.

'Please may David and Jenny stay the night?' continued Jo. 'We want to have a talk.'

'What about?'

'How I can get on better at school.'

'I see.' Mr Grant stared at them, rather taken aback. 'What about your parents?' he asked.

'They'll be OK,' David said casually. He was never any good at talking to adults and Jenny wished that she had got in first.

Mr Grant, however, didn't seem to notice. 'It's good of you both,' he muttered. 'I've been worried about Jo ever since her mum died. She was only a toddler and she hasn't been well over the last few years.'

'It's all right, Dad. I've told them all about that.'

'Have you?' He seemed rather put out, as if his daughter had been giving away family secrets. Then his gratitude won. 'Jo needs friends. She was badly bullied at her other school too.'

Jo quickly interrupted him. 'I told you, Dad. Jenny and David know all about me.'

'Of course. Well, providing your parents have given permission I'd be delighted if you'd both stay the night. David can have the couch down here, if you don't mind sharing Jo's room, Jenny.'

'That'll be fine.' It was all falling nicely into place, Jenny thought.

'You'll be welcome. I'm sorry it's such a small place, but I was made redundant last year and I've only just started up again with a new company.' Mr Grant laughed bitterly. 'I don't suppose my ancestor would have thought much of me. It's my mother's side of the family that's got the money and they haven't been very generous to me and Jo. We're nearly on our uppers.' Bob Grant paused reflectively. 'I always mean to get the Council to give me access to that old folly for an hour or two. Even the Fairfaxes couldn't save the house, and the tower looks so stranded and dilapidated stuck in that rundown park. Typical of the local authority. No imagination at all.' Then he seemed to remember Jo and her problem. 'Now what's been happening?'

As Jo finished telling her father about Barry Workman, she said, 'David and Jenny really backed me up, Dad, and I'm not afraid of him any longer. It's good to have friends. At last.'

Jenny broke in at that point, wishing Barry was the only problem. She'd rather face dozens of school bullies than a flock of birds with a hostile instinct. 'We'll back Jo any time,' she said. 'She's going to join some school clubs – and come on the next outing.'

'If I can afford it,' said Bob Grant gloomily.

Then he brightened. 'But I'm sure I can. Jo needs a bit of a leg up,' he told them. 'Now, how about some tea?'

CHAPTER SEVEN

David lay awake on the sofa, listening to the night. The evening had been rather tense, and although they had watched TV, with Mr Grant hovering like a butler in the background, seeing to their every need, the minutes had crawled past like hours. He had felt the birds' presence everywhere and had several times thought he heard their beaks tapping urgently against the window panes.

He was sure that Jenny was equally uneasy, but Jo seemed withdrawn, as if she was fading away, drawing back into her own private world again. Before they had gone to bed, however, Jo had come up to him, her eyes full of fear.

'Jenny will stay with me all the time, won't she?'

'Of course she will,' he had reassured her.

'Where do you think I'm going? For a walk?' Jenny had said. But her flippant remark had somehow made Jo even more nervous.

As David drifted into sleep, he dreamt they were back in the tower, racing up the cobweb-hung spiral staircase, while the birds waited on the landing, riding an enormous rocking chair that was empty of any human being but filled with a black mass of seething feathers and reddened, angry, nugget eyes.

He was wakened by the repeated call of an owl, unusual to hear in London. Reluctantly he got off the sofa and went to the window, drawing the curtains aside. The crescent moon lit a frosty front garden and the surrounding rows of box-like dwellings that made up the estate. Some of the houses were still under construction, and mounds of raw earth, cement mixers and half-finished walls were silvered with frost, turning the building site into what seemed like a glistening fairytale city, transforming its bland ugliness into a semblance of beauty.

Then David started and gazed out disbelievingly at what he thought at first must be a trick of the light. On top of one of the piles of earth was a wooden cradle, gleaming with hoar frost. The owl's talons were rocking the cradle to and fro, while from inside came the muffled wail of a baby.

Panic filled him. Could the creaking in the Dark

Tower have been caused by a cradle and not a rocking chair? The sound seemed to fill his head. He had to get upstairs, but now he seemed rooted to the sitting-room carpet.

He tried to move, but the thick pile refused to let him go. Suddenly he felt himself sinking, and the more he struggled, the tighter he was held, while the owl's hooting became increasingly urgent and menacing.

Upstairs, Jenny and Jo had also been wakened by the hooting and when Jenny opened the curtains they both saw exactly what David had seen – the owl rocking the cradle as gently as any loving mother on the frost-covered mound of earth.

The baby's crying was intermittent, frail and uneven, and then they heard a wheezing sound. The wailing started up again, but it was weaker now, barely a thread of sound.

'It's amazing,' whispered Jenny. She didn't understand what she was seeing but it scared her. 'Is that what you heard? The baby crying?'

'Not like that,' Jo hissed, her whole body tense. 'There's something wrong. He's ill.'

'Why *he*?'

'I don't know.'

'Who *is* he?'

'Someone close to me.'

'Is that what you used to dream about?' asked Jenny in bewilderment. 'An owl rocking a cradle?'

'No. I just used to hear the baby. I never *saw* anything. This isn't a dream, though. It can't be. We're sharing it. That couldn't happen, could it?'

'It might,' said Jenny cautiously.

This is like a nightmare, thought David. The carpet still seemed to be pulling him down yet an inner sense of urgency, of danger, made him keep trying to move.

The sitting room looked normal enough, and when David reached out he could feel the tough leather of a battered armchair. He knocked over a cup as he fell to the floor and cold coffee crept over the carpet.

Something moved under Jo's bed. For a moment, the two girls froze, refusing to believe they had heard anything. Then the movement came again, rather like a scuffling and a scratching mixed up together.

'Do you keep cats?' whispered Jenny hopefully.

'We don't have any pets.'

'Could a cat have got in?'

'It doesn't sound like a cat,' said Jo bleakly. 'It sounds more like a—' But she couldn't bring herself to say the word.

Neither could Jenny, and they gazed at each other in creeping horror.

The scratching and scuffling came again, louder this time. Then Jenny saw the yellow beak sticking out from under the bed.

'Birds,' hissed Jo.

'How did they get there? The window's closed.'

'They must have flown up the landing.'

'From where?'

They were still talking in whispers.

Jenny measured the distance to the door. They could cover it in a couple of strides.

'Maybe Dad left the back door open.' Jo paused and then gave a little whimpering cry. 'Is he all right? Do you think my dad's all right? The birds – they couldn't have hurt him—'

They both ran for the door at the same time, only to find that it was slowly opening.

Jo began to scream.

David began to crawl to the door. Slowly, but only very slowly, he made progress and eventually dragged himself up, pulled the door open and staggered out into the hall. There was a snapping sound and he was free and back to normal.

When he gazed back into the room, all David could see was a dirty green, threadbare carpet with an upturned coffee cup and a slight stain. Not knowing whether he was awake or not, he ran to the foot of the stairs and heard Jenny and Jo screaming.

Birds were everywhere. Some came from the landing, others from the open door of Jo's bedroom. Some were perched on the banisters and more were hovering near the ceiling, their wings beating noisily. Suddenly they all rose and began to fly down the stairs in formation, a black cloud that blotted out the light.

For a moment they mobbed David, flapping in his face, and he could smell their acrid bodies as they streaked towards the kitchen. Flailing his arms he fell over again, rolling on to his stomach, covering his face, kicking out at nothing but space.

When he rolled over again, David could see Jenny and Jo standing at the top of the stairs, gazing down at him numbly.

'Are you OK?'

'Are *you*?' David gasped as he rose unsteadily to his feet.

'They were in the bedroom,' said Jenny. 'Rooks. They must have crept under the bed while we were asleep.' She shuddered.

'Did you see the owl and the cradle?'

'We saw them,' Jenny replied bleakly, but Jo had already run into the adjoining bedroom and was only in there for a few seconds before she emerged again, her face chalk white.

'Dad!' she was screaming.

'What about him?' demanded David.

'He's not in his bed.'

Jo began to run down the stairs, almost colliding with David as she headed straight for the kitchen, followed by a frantic Jenny. When he joined them, David could see they were kneeling down.

Bob Grant lay still on the lino. The birds had gone and the kitchen door was half open. To their relief he slowly began to stir and sat up, groaning.

'I opened the door,' he muttered.

'Why?' Jo demanded.

'There was scratching. Then they came in. They flew in.'

'Did they attack you?'

'No. They just went past me in a great black cloud. Then I must have fallen over and hit my head on the table. Or was I dreaming?' He looked bewildered, unsure of himself.

Jenny could see that there was bright red blood in Mr Grant's hair, but it didn't seem to be oozing and some of it was dry. She wondered how long he had been lying there.

'No,' said David. 'You weren't dreaming.'

'But I've never seen birds fly into a house before. Not like that. So many of them. As if they were seeking sanctuary.' Bob Grant shook his head, as if he didn't really believe what he was saying.

'It's cold out there,' said Jenny.

'Not that cold.'

'There's a terrific frost.' David was suddenly anxious to bring things back to normal, to reassure Jo's father. Instinctively he knew that they had to keep the true situation to themselves.

'They came in for *warmth*?' Mr Grant was incredulous. 'That's a pretty stupid idea, isn't it?' Although he didn't believe David's theory, he seemed too shocked to pursue any others.

'Maybe they're starving,' Jenny suggested.

'Where are they now?'

'They flew out again.'

Mr Grant rubbed at the back of his head. 'There'll be droppings everywhere.'

'I haven't seen any,' said David.

'You ought to go to hospital, Dad.' Jo sounded anxious.

'Nonsense!' He seemed to get stronger at the very mention of the idea. 'I've got a long journey tomorrow.'

'Let's have a look,' volunteered David. 'My sister and I have done a First Aid course.'

'So have I,' said Mr Grant impatiently. 'Mark you – it was years ago.'

'You won't be able to see what you're doing.' Jo was dismissive. 'Let Jenny and David help you.'

David cleaned the shallow cut and put on a piece of sticking plaster. Much to Mr Grant's surprise he wasn't clumsy at all. Then, glancing in the mirror that was on the wall in front of her, Jenny saw a reflection that caught her attention. She took a longer look and just managed to stop herself screaming. It *couldn't* be. But it was. She was gazing at the edge of a cradle, and when she grabbed David's arm and swung him round he saw it too. Then it shimmered away into nothing at all.

Bob Grant made hot chocolate, and they sat round the kitchen table trying to recover while they debated the cause of the birds' attack. But while they talked, Jenny, David and Jo longed to be alone together, to try and understand the real implications of it all.

'I'm going to ring up the local radio,' said Mr Grant. 'I bet you nothing like that has ever happened before.' He sounded quite excited now he had got over the shock.

'Maybe the radio will contact some local ornithologist, Dad,' suggested Jo. 'There must be some reason. Perhaps they *were* starving.' She wanted to make the invasion logical for him.

'Enough to invade a house?' Mr Grant paused. 'They were mainly rooks, weren't they?'

Jenny nodded and David yawned. 'There's no point in speculating. I must get some sleep or I'll really mess up school tomorrow.'

'You don't think they'll come back, do you?' Jo asked fearfully, seeking a reassurance no one could give her.

'Not if I can help it,' said her father fiercely. He put a chair against the door and then glanced at the windows. 'They're double-glazed. They won't let that lot through.'

They'll get through anything if they want to, thought David.

Waiting until they were sure Mr Grant had been back in bed for some time, Jenny and Jo crept downstairs and into the darkened sitting room so they could talk to David. They were all three completely wide awake and knew that there was no point in even trying to sleep until they had properly discussed the invasion.

'I'm sure they're trying to communicate something,' whispered David. 'But why should they be so hostile?'

'Communicate what?' asked Jenny.

'I don't know, but it must be something to do with the Dark Tower.' He paused uncertainly. 'And you, Jo.'

'What else do you know about Sir James?' asked Jenny.

Jo tried to get a grip on herself. 'Nothing beyond what I've told you. He loved birds. He loved travel. He built the folly. Then he infected his wife and baby son with typhoid. They died.'

'But what happened to Sir James?' hissed David urgently. 'You said he went abroad. Are you sure about that?'

'No. I don't know anything else about him. Nothing at all.'

'Haven't you ever asked your dad?'

'Of course. But he doesn't know either.'

'Are you sure?' whispered Jenny. 'Are you sure he's not keeping anything back from you?'

'Why should he?'

'He'd be worried about frightening you. After all – you're—'

'The nervy type,' muttered Jo.

'I'll ask him at breakfast,' promised David.

'Be careful,' said Jenny. 'Maybe it would be better if I did.'

'No,' David snapped, tired and irritable. 'You're always trying to take over. Let me handle it for a change.'

'All right,' sighed Jenny. 'But remember what I said. Be careful.'

They dozed fitfully for the rest of the night, waking every now and then, thinking they heard a rattling at the windowpane or a soft rustling of feathers on the stairs. Jo snuggled down in bed, pulling the covers over her head and whimpering several times, while Jenny went at least twice to the window, gazing out at the frost-shrouded estate. But there was no sign of an owl or a cradle, and although she opened the window a crack Jenny couldn't hear a baby crying. Only the sound of frost crackling.

Downstairs, David did much the same, staring out at the estate and then returning to the kitchen, checking that the back door was firmly bolted and the chairback was still firmly wedged under the handle. He double-checked several times, listening to the low hum of the fridge, waiting for other more ominous sounds but hearing nothing more.

He went back to the sofa and lay down, closing his eyes and drifting into unsettled dreams where birds swooped and wheeled and dived, regally presided over by an owl, rocking a cradle.

David was first in the kitchen, hanging about until Mr Grant appeared, his face strained and his eyes glazed, looking just as bad as David felt.

'Couldn't you sleep?' he asked as he filled the kettle and set it shakily on the stove.

'Not very well.'

'Hardly surprising.'

They were silent for a while until David said, 'That was weird.'

'Last night's bird flight.' Bob Grant laughed huskily. 'I've decided to phone a vet. Someone who knows about animals. The radio will only send reporters round here.'

'Yes.' David wondered if he should offer to be useful. 'Shall I lay the table?'

'I can do that. Why don't you call the girls?'

'I think they're getting ready.' He poised himself for the plunge. It was going to be awkward either way. Surely even Jenny would have found that. 'Er – you know how kind your ancestor was to the birds in the Dark Tower.'

'Sir James. He was dotty about them. But I don't suppose they invaded the Hall like they did the house last night. I'm certain it was the cold. They saw a warm light and—'

'How did Sir James die?'

Mr Grant gazed at him suspiciously. 'I've no idea,' he replied abruptly.

'I just wondered.' David knew he was being too nonchalant.

'All I know is that Sir James left after his son Peter died.'

Just then Jo clattered into the kitchen followed by Jenny. 'You doing a fry-up, Dad? I'm starving. And how's your head?' She seemed amazingly bright after the disturbed night. David and Mr Grant stared back at her blankly and immediately she was suspicious. 'What are you two on about?' she demanded. 'Sharing secrets? Is there any more news on the birds?'

'We're not doing anything of the kind and there's no news,' said Bob Grant firmly. 'And if you *do* want a fry-up, get some knives and forks on the table and stop asking questions!'

CHAPTER EIGHT

David, Jenny and Jo walked through the freezing streets to school, black ice underfoot and a thin, cutting wind numbing their hands and feet. The sky was steel grey with the hard outline of a cold sun on the distant horizon.

Jo was quiet, only occasionally asking for reassurance. 'You won't let me be on my own,' she had pleaded at least twice, and David and Jenny had assured her that this wouldn't happen. But they both wondered what they were going to do. Suppose the situation wasn't resolved? They couldn't move in with Jo indefinitely, thought Jenny. Nor could she come and stay with them for too long a period.

David's exhaustion had made his normal optimism fade. They had become Jo's guardians, and although he liked and wanted to help her, he was also afraid.

Halfway through English, Jenny passed David a note which read WHAT DID YOU FIND OUT – IF ANYTHING?

Annoyed by his sister's assumption that he had failed to get Mr Grant to communicate, he wrote back in equally big capital letters: SIR JAMES LEFT BECAUSE HIS SON PETER DIED.

Unfortunately, David gave the note to his best friend Alan Watkins to pass back to Jenny. He had forgotten how reckless Alan could be and when he remembered it was too late to stop him flicking the note at her. His aim was as bad as usual and the scrap of paper landed on the floor between the desks. Worse still, it was seen by Mr Parks, the English teacher, who was insistent that there should be no communication of any sort between his students while they listened to his every golden word.

'Did you flick something, Watkins?'

'No, sir.'

'I think you did.'

'I didn't, sir.'

'Your aim is as poor as ever, isn't it, Watkins?'

'Is it, sir?'

'Get me that piece of paper.'

Grimly, Alan bent down, retrieved David's

message and walked slowly up to the front of the class.

'You seem reluctant,' observed Mr Parks, opening the folded-up paper and reading out sarcastically, 'Sir James left because his son Peter died.' He paused, gazing down at Alan blandly. 'I don't understand,' he said. 'Can you enlighten me?'

David glanced across at Jenny, who was glaring at him, and then at Jo, who was looking uncomfortable.

'Playing the detective, are you, Watkins?'

'Er—'

'Can you tell me a little more about Sir James?'

'That's my note, sir. Not Alan's.' David stood up. He could see the whole class turning round to gaze at the sacrificial victim. Barry Workman, in particular, was looking delighted.

'I see. Well – I'm waiting for an explanation.'

David was usually inventive but this time his mind had gone blank.

'Er—'

'Yes?'

Barry drew a finger across his thick neck in morbid satisfaction.

Jenny closed her eyes. Was David going to blurt everything out? She stole a covert glance at Jo and saw her eyes were fixed on David, obviously afraid of what he might say.

'I haven't got one, sir.'

'See me afterwards for a detention.'

David sat down, not in the least worried about his detention, but extremely concerned about Jo and how he might have upset her. After all that had happened, he didn't dare to catch her eye, but he did catch Barry's, and flinched at his look of sneering triumph.

CHAPTER NINE

'You idiot.' Jenny had searched out her twin during break, to find him shame-faced and guilty. 'You raving idiot!'

'I'm sorry.'

'You should be.'

'Where's Jo?'

'Being brave.'

'What now then?'

'I've had an idea,' said Jenny, relenting slightly, for she knew how much David was suffering. 'We need to find out a bit more about the Dark Tower. Like talk to a local historian and I think I know just the man.'

'Who?' demanded David miserably.

'The head of History,' said Jenny. 'Mr Dutton. Someone once told me he knows everything there is to know about this part of the East End.'

'Including Fairfax Park?'

'I hope so.' Jenny grinned at him. 'Don't worry, Dave. It was just a mistake.'

'A clumsy one. Are you sure I haven't really upset Jo?'

'I don't care if you have,' Jenny replied brutally. 'She's got to face facts. Whatever's happening in the Dark Tower is linked to her family. I'm sure the birds want her – not us.'

'Maybe they want to kill Jo,' said David bleakly. 'We've got to look after her.'

'We'll do all we can. But I don't think they want to hurt her. I'm beginning to wonder if Jo is the key to some – problem.'

David nodded. 'You mean she can make something happen for them?'

'It must have something to do with that baby in the cradle.'

He considered what she had said carefully. 'But what are these birds up to? Do they want Jo to help the baby? It must be the ghost of Sir James's baby – the one who died of typhoid.'

'I reckon they want her to do something they can't. Something only she can do. That's why they want us out of the way.'

'So you think the birds came into the Grants' house to warn us to lay off?'

'I think they came to fetch Jo.'

'And we stopped her going with them? That must have annoyed them.' David looked apprehensive.

'Don't forget birds can only work by instinct. The instinct of thousands of years. Handed down, like an inheritance.'

'So we're all in danger. Jo because she has to do some kind of awful task. And us because we're trying to protect her.'

Jenny nodded.

'Do you think you can find out more from Mr Dutton?'

'If we know the full history of the tower, then we've got more of a chance of helping her.'

'*How* can you help me?' Jo's voice was eager as she came up behind the twins. There was a much more resolute expression on her face. 'What are you up to?' She grinned. 'Plotting?'

'No,' replied Jenny, taken off guard and knowing she sounded unconvincing.

'You're not going to start leaving me out, are you?' Jo looked worried now. 'You've both got to realise that the birds don't want you – it's only me they're after so I need to toughen up. Dad's been spoiling me for years. Whatever happens, I need to see this through. So what *were* you talking about?'

'Mr Dutton. Head of History,' said Jenny. 'He's a local historian and might know more about the tower. I'm going to make an appointment with him.'

'There's nothing else?' she asked suspiciously.

'No.' David was firm. 'We're all in this together – and we're going to see it through. Together.'

Jenny poked her head tentatively around the door of Mr Dutton's office at lunchtime.

He was a small man with a large head which gave him an almost gnome-like appearance. He always wore a dark suit, white shirt and the same polka-dot bow tie. Jenny liked him because he was different from the other teachers, not just in the way he dressed but in his attitude. If a pupil was interested in his subject he spoke to them as an equal. If not, he ignored them. Jenny had always got on with Mr Dutton.

'Yes, Jenny? How can I help you?'

She came straight to the point. 'My brother and I cycle past that folly in Fairfax Park every day and we were wondering what its history was.'

'The Dark Tower?' Mr Dutton beamed at her in anticipation of imparting knowledge and then looked down at his watch. 'We've got twenty minutes. Why don't you come in and sit down? And how about a chocolate biscuit?'

'Am I interrupting?' She looked at the pile of pupils' books lying on his desk.

'No.' He laughed. 'You're liberating me. Close that door and ask me any questions you like. The Dark Tower is a fascinating subject – if a tragic one.'

As David kicked a football about with some friends, Barry Workman made a triumphant appearance.

'That served you right, Golding,' he said. 'Fancy sending stupid notes like that. What are you doing? Making up some babyish story?'

If only you knew how frightening babies could be, thought David. But he had been expecting Barry and was determined not to lose his temper. 'I've got a story to tell you. It's all about a real prat who interrupted a game of football. Do you know what happened to him?' The other players were moving behind David now. Barry Workman wasn't exactly popular.

'No.' He was getting uneasy.

'Well, it's not such a good story really because it's got a very obvious ending. You see, what happened is this: these kids played football every day in the playground but they never had a goal mouth. Nothing to really aim at. Know what I mean?'

Sensing the danger he was in, Barry decided to run. But he wasn't fast enough for David who placed the ball, moved into position and kicked it hard at his large backside. The impact and subsequent howl of pain had everyone in the playground wincing.

'Nice shot,' said someone.

Jenny munched chocolate biscuits and relaxed slightly as Mr Dutton talked. It was as if he was discussing a dusty old legend rather than a real danger that wasn't going to go away.

'Sir James picked up a mild dose of typhoid on his travels. It wasn't fatal to him, but he infected his wife and put his baby son at risk.'

'Did he *know* he'd become a carrier?' asked Jenny.

'The doctors guessed that was what had happened. But of course medicine was even less of an exact science then than it is today. Sir James's baby son Peter was still alive and so far unaffected. So he quarantined him in the Dark Tower.'

'Who looked after him?'

'He had a nurse named Anna Wolff – a faithful old servant who had been with the family for years. For a while it looked as if the baby was going to survive. Then Peter suddenly contracted the disease and despite everyone's efforts died a few days later. Sir James was heartbroken and he died soon afterwards.'

'What happened to Anna Wolff?'

'She apparently never left her cottage again. The Fairfax family supported Anna until her death. It was all a terrible tragedy.' Mr Dutton paused. 'You know Sir James is an ancestor of Josephine Grant's?'

Jenny nodded. 'She's a friend of mine. That's why I'm asking really. She'd like to know more as well.'

'She's always welcome to come and talk to me.'

'Jo's a bit shy.'

'So I've noticed.'

'What about the birds? Didn't Sir James befriend them or something?'

Clive Dutton frowned. 'You don't want to mix up fact with fiction. All I've told you is in the Fairfax family records that are kept in the Denton Street Museum. You can go and check them yourself if you like. But there's no mention of birds.'

Jenny was disappointed. 'You mean it's all untrue?'

'It's simply oral history. What's been passed down by word of mouth.'

'So it's a pack of lies.'

'I didn't say that, Jenny. But it's not reliable.'

'Do you know about the birds?'

'Yes. The legend goes that Sir James had some kind of magical relationship with the birds. But we're talking about myth. I did see in the records that he used to have nesting boxes on the outside of the tower as well as food. Birds were beyond being a hobby. They were his passion.' He looked at her curiously. 'Now you can tell me something.'

'Yes of course. If I can.' Jenny was slightly thrown.

'Jo Grant. She's very nervous, isn't she?'

'Yes.'

'You're good friends?'

'That's right.'

'Hasn't she been ill?'

'Yes.' Jenny was wary now.

'Do you think she's getting worked up about the Dark Tower and the family connection?'

'I think she may be.' She was guarded.

Mr Dutton sighed. 'I wish I was on the pastoral

staff here. I'd like to talk to her. Are *you* trying to help?'

'Me and my brother, David. We're both trying, sir.'

'You will discourage her from believing in legends, won't you, Jenny? The facts stand up for themselves. The myths don't.'

You'd be surprised, she thought. 'David and I are just trying to be good friends to Jo.'

Mr Dutton nodded and reluctantly drew forward the tall pile of exercise books.

He doesn't understand. He's too rational, thought Jenny. Then she felt a sudden stab of fear. If only Mr Dutton *could* understand.

'You'll come back and see me if I can give any more assistance?' he asked hesitantly.

'Of course I will, sir.'

Suddenly Jenny felt very alone.

'So why are the birds trying to trap me?' said Jo as they talked in the bike shed after Jenny had told them both what Mr Dutton had said. She looked exhausted and much of her former resolution seemed to have disappeared. 'Why was I drawn to the tower in the first place? Why me?' she demanded, and both David and Jenny knew that she had become even more dependent on them. 'No wonder Dad kept all this a secret.' She paused. 'I wish he hadn't though.'

'I reckon it's because you're family,' said David. 'Because someone needs you. Maybe it's the baby,' he added doubtfully.

'Why should the baby need me? He's dead.'

The twins were silent.

'These family records,' said David suddenly. 'Do you think they could tell us any more about Sir James's death? What time does that museum in Denton Street close?'

'We can't be that late home. We stayed out all last night and you've already had detention. Mum and Dad will think we don't want to see them.'

'I'll go,' said Jo. 'I'll go to the museum on my own.'

The twins looked at her doubtfully. 'Are you sure?' asked Jenny.

'I've got to face up to it all. It's my responsibility.'

'It's ours too,' said David. 'Not just yours. And what about the Dark Tower? You'll pass it on your way home and it might—'

'I'll go back another way,' she said fiercely.

'Suppose you're compelled to go inside again?'

Jenny asked.

'It's only when I've gone *past* the park that I've found myself going inside. So I'll go the long way round. But if it makes you feel any better I'll ring Dad and ask him to come and pick me up from the museum. I'll say I had to do some research for a homework project and he'll come and fetch me in the car. That way I'll be completely safe.'

David still looked doubtful, but Jenny was sure their parents would be both angry and upset if they stayed away any longer. 'We've got to go home, Dave,' she said.

'OK.' He was reluctant. 'But you ring us, Jo. Call us directly you get back home.'

'All right.'

'You promise?'

'I promise. I've just got to find out why the birds want me so much.'

'You *must* stay by the museum until your dad comes,' Jenny insisted.

'OK.' Jo was almost irritable. 'I can look after myself.'

But both Jenny and David knew that this was the one thing she couldn't do.

CHAPTER TEN

At home the twins received a predictably cool reception.

'You look terrible,' said Mrs Golding as they arrived in the kitchen, suddenly incredibly hungry but still uneasy about Jo. 'What were you doing last night?'

'Talking,' David replied sullenly.

'Is that all?'

'That's it.'

She turned to Jenny. 'And you were talking as well?'

'Yes. Sorry, Mum.'

'I warned you about sitting up late.' Mrs Golding glanced at her watch. 'And you're not exactly early now.'

'I got a detention.' David decided to confess immediately, before his mother wormed it out of him.

'What did I say?' She was full of indignation and 'told-you-so' reproach. 'You're up all night and expect to cope with school.'

'Sorry, Mum.' David decided to take Jenny's line. Anyway, he was too tired to do anything else.

'I should think so. And by the way – that Jo. I've been hearing about her.'

'Who from?' said Jenny shortly, not liking her mother's tone.

'From Mrs Jessop. I met her in the supermarket. She's got a son in your year.'

'Frank Jessop,' said David, saying the name with considerable distaste. 'He's a mate of Barry Workman's.'

Mrs Golding ignored him. 'She was saying that this Jo's a peculiar sort of girl. Disturbed, she said.'

David was about to reply when Jenny intervened. She wasn't going to let anyone get away with that – even her mother. 'Don't you listen to her,' she snapped. 'Jo's a lovely person. She just wants a bit of support, that's all. And friendship.'

'We're Jo's friends, Mum,' said David bluntly. 'We have to back her up.'

An hour later, while the twins were up in their bedrooms doing their homework and trying not to fall asleep, Mrs Golding came up the stairs and banged on their doors.

'It's your friend Jo,' she announced indignantly. 'She's on the phone. In hysterics.'

David and Jenny thundered downstairs full of trepidation and Jenny grabbed the phone.

'What is it, Jo.'

'He was waiting for me.' There was a sob in her voice.

'Who?' Jenny felt deeply afraid, as if she was being threatened herself.

'The owl.'

'Don't be daft. Where are you?' She tried desperately to stay calm.

'In a telephone box.'

Jenny glanced out of the window. The wind had dropped, freezing fog had descended and the visibility was down to less than a metre.

'What happened?' she asked, while David hunched up close to her, trying to listen as well.

'I went to the museum and I – I found out where Sir James is buried.'

'Where?'

'Near the tower in unconsecrated ground. But I also found out something else.' Jo hesitated and Jenny almost shouted down the line, 'What *is* it?'

'Sir James committed suicide – that's why he wasn't allowed to be buried in a churchyard. Taking your own life is a sin – the owl – the thing's staring at me. I went to this phone box to ring Dad and—'

'Where is it?' interrupted Jenny.

'In a side street, near the museum.' She paused and they could hear her crying. 'The owl's outside sitting on a tree. I can just see him in the fog. He's *still* staring at me.'

'He can't hurt you. Just walk away. Go back to the museum.'

'I can't.' Jo began to sob. 'He's – it's like he's looking right though me. Into my mind. He wants to take me back to the Dark Tower.'

'He can't hurt you.' But already Jenny was condemning herself for letting Jo go to the museum on her own and she could see that David was feeling exactly the same.

'You've got to help me!' Jo's voice was high and she sounded as if she was on the verge of losing control.

'Phone your father. Get him to pick you up right away.'

'You don't understand!'

'Don't understand what?'

'The rooks are coming. There's two already.

Now a third. They're in the branches of the tree with him. Two rooks. And now a crow.'

'All right.' Jenny managed to make her voice completely reassuring. 'We're coming now. Stay in the telephone box.'

'Suppose someone wants to use it?'

'Just stay there. We'll be with you in a few minutes. OK?'

'OK.' Jo's voice was small and despairing.

Jenny slammed down the receiver and turned to David. 'Did you hear all that? About Sir Ja—'

'I heard,' snapped David. 'We've got to get to her. Now!'

They ran back into the hall and grabbed their coats. Then Jenny said, 'I'll tell Mum.'

'She'll go crazy.'

'I've still got to tell her.' She hurried down to the kitchen and opened the door. 'Mum . . .'

'Do you want some hot chocolate?' Mrs Golding sounded penitent, as if she realised how unfairly she had talked about Jo, little realising that Jenny was about to put her to the test.

'Jo's in trouble.'

'Trouble?'

'She's got – locked in a telephone box and she's crying her eyes out.'

'A telephone box doesn't *have* a lock.'

'I think she's being bullied.'

'Where is she?'

'Near Denton Street Museum.'

'Do you want me to drive you over?' Mrs Golding was partly indignant, partly concerned. Her concern was winning.

'No. We'll go over on our bikes. Thanks all the same.'

'But the fog—'

'We know the way backwards.'

'I can't have you—'

'We'll be all right, Mum.' Then Jenny remembered about the car. 'And didn't you say the clutch was slipping. That would be even *more* dangerous. Going out in the fog with a slipping clutch. Someone in front of us might brake suddenly and—'

'All right. Off you go. But don't be long and keep in touch.' Mrs Golding paused. 'Why don't you bring Jo back with you if her father doesn't mind? She sounds a nervous little thing and I've got some home-made soup on the go and there's some of that lemon curd tart still in the larder. She wants feeding up.'

Jenny threw her arms around her mother, kissing her on both cheeks. 'You are lovely, Mum.'

'Be careful,' warned Mrs Golding.

The fog was so dense that the lights on David and Jenny's bikes hardly penetrated its thick grey strands. Sounds seemed distorted, but fortunately the traffic went past them at a crawling pace. Occasionally they heard a voice or the muffled hum of a car engine, sometimes close, sometimes at a great distance and then near again.

The twins pedalled along as fast as they dared and at last arrived at the museum, pausing uncertainly and gazing round desperately.

'What now?' asked Jenny.

The museum was on the junction of two narrow side streets and a long, busy main road. To their frustration they couldn't immediately see a telephone box, and then suddenly they both saw its sign dimly shining.

'Let's try that one,' said David, and they cycled on slowly, wobbling past a line of parked cars.

'There she is!' said Jenny in relief. 'She's still inside.'

The twins pulled their bikes up on to the pavement, leant them against a wall and strode towards the telephone box. There was no sign of any birds. David threw open the door and yelled, 'Jo. It's all right. We're here! You're safe!'

'Who do you think you are?' shouted the woman. 'Get out. This is a private conversation!'

'I'm sorry,' said David, completely taken aback. 'We're looking for a friend. Have you seen her?'

'No, I haven't seen anyone. Go away.'

David closed the door and turned to Jenny. 'Now what?'

She gazed hopelessly round her. 'Wait a minute. There's a man selling newspapers over there. He may have seen Jo.'

The twins hurried over to a surly-looking news vendor with a balaclava and thick woollen mittens. The man *had* to help, but he looked very grumpy.

'I'm sorry,' said Jenny politely. 'We've lost our friend.'

'Yeah?'

'She called us from that phone box – and now she's gone.'

The man stared at her, his face expressionless, and then turned away to sell a newspaper. Someone else came up, fumbling for money.

'What was you saying?' the man grumbled as the fog seemed to close in even more densely than before.

'This friend of ours. She's only young. She – she got lost in the fog and phoned us from that box. Her name's Jo – Jo Grant – and she was terrified. Did you see her?' pleaded Jenny.

The man's expression softened. 'Was she the little lassie with the owl?'

'*What*?' David was incredulous and Jenny's stomach gave a lurch as if she was suddenly shooting down in a lift.

'I haven't seen a pet owl in years. Did she rescue it?'

Jenny nodded. 'What happened?' Her mouth was so dry she could hardly bring out the words.

'She came out of the phone box with the owl on her shoulder. I only saw her because she passed so close to the stand. But she was going at quite a pace – almost running she was. As if she had an appointment like.'

The twins knew where the appointment would be.

CHAPTER ELEVEN

David and Jenny reached Fairfax Park ten minutes later, only to find the gates still open. Obviously the council couldn't be bothered to close them.

Looking round to make sure they weren't seen and welcoming the fog for the first time, the twins hid their bikes in the bushes, took off their lights, hurried inside the gates and gazed about them. The landscape was masked by swirling bands of freezing fog and the oaks looked like the spars of some giant ship drifting through a vast lake, while the top of the Dark Tower, looming in and out of the murk, seemed to hover above a bank of cloud.

As they drew nearer, the twins saw that the door was once again half open.

'Let's go inside,' said David. 'Jo might be in there.'

'OK,' Jenny replied uneasily. 'We'd—' She broke off as they both heard a low moan.

'There's someone round the back of the tower,' she whispered. 'Listen.'

They strained their ears, and after a while heard a faint groaning sound.

Their bike lights made little impression on the fog as the twins edged their way round the ivy-hung walls of the tower. The stuff was unpleasant to the touch, with wiry stems and slippery leaves.

Suddenly, an owl screeched and flew up into their faces, talons almost brushing their heads and partly hooded eyes blazing an angry red.

Then it was gone, lost in the fog, and the ivy rustled menacingly.

'They don't want us,' whispered Jenny. 'They only want Jo.'

'But who are *they*?' demanded David. 'The birds? Or is there some other force operating here?'

The groan came again, this time much more strongly, and the twins pressed on, their fear increasing, terrified of what they might find.

Behind the tower was a thicket of dead-looking brambles and more trails of ivy that ran along the ground and clustered around what looked like a hummock covered in bird droppings.

Lying beside it was Jo, with a cut on her head

almost identical to her father's, looking as if the skin had been broken by a beak.

'Maybe she resisted them,' said Jenny, kneeling down by Jo and stroking her face tenderly.

Slowly Jo's eyes opened and she shifted a little in the ivy and brambles.

'I knew you'd find me,' she muttered. 'I knew you'd come.'

'What happened?' demanded Jenny.

'I opened the door of the phone box and the owl came in with me and sat on my shoulder. Its beak kept nudging my cheek. I knew where I had to go.'

'Didn't you fight back?' asked David.

'I tried. That's why he attacked me.' Jo's voice was a monotone. 'The owl led me to this grave. It's Sir James's.' She sat up and began to push back the strands of ivy which unwillingly revealed mossy lettering. At first it was hard to decipher. David shone his cycle light on the old gravestone. Then, haltingly, he read the inscription aloud:

'IN LOVING MEMORY OF SIR JAMES FAIRFAX
HE LIVED FOR HIS FAMILY
HE DIED WITHOUT THEM
NOT EVEN HIS BIRDS COULD PROTECT HIM'

There were more letters, hastily scratched below; David worked the moss off them.

'I ALONE HAVE THE KNOWLEDGE TO RESTORE
HIS NAME TO THE RIGHTFUL PLACE. A.W.'

'What does "rightful place" mean?' asked Jenny.

'It must be about this consecrated ground thing,' replied David. 'But what is it A.W. knows that no one else does?'

'I've got to go into the tower,' said Jo, rising slowly and painfully to her feet. 'I've got to get it over. If I don't, they'll never stop hunting me down.'

'Not without us, you don't,' said David firmly.

'I've got to go now.' Her eyes were glazed as she stared at the ivy-hung walls.

The cut on Jo's head looked deeper than her father's, and she had definitely been unconscious. Surely she should be checked for concussion, thought Jenny.

'We'll go into the tower again tomorrow,' suggested David. 'We need to get you to a hospital.'

Jo shook her head. 'I *have* to go, and you can't come with me. They don't want you.'

'Too bad,' replied David. 'The birds are going to have to put up with us.'

They edged their way back round the tower. David checked his watch. It was 9 p.m. and he knew their mother would already be worrying, but there was no way out. They *had* to help Jo confront the tower, whatever the consequences. They couldn't possibly leave her to face the birds on her own.

The fog seemed even thicker now and they could barely see. Jenny pushed at the half-opened door of the tower but it suddenly slammed shut like a gunshot in the velvet silence. The fog spread like a blanket that threatened to reach down their throats and suffocate them.

Jenny tried the door, but it seemed to have locked itself.

'Let me have a go,' said Jo.

Reluctantly the twins stood back as she placed a trembling hand on the latch.

The door swung open, immediately emitting the dank, shut-in smell that had alarmed them so much before.

The beams from their lamps swept the cob-webbed gloom, picking out the spiral staircase. As far as they could see there were no birds. Nor was there the slightest sound of them and they all felt a sense of anti-climax.

'It's their night off,' said David in relief, trying to be funny.

Jo began to walk slowly towards the staircase. Then she stopped. 'I should go up,' she said, not moving at all.

'We'll come with you.' Jenny was determined. 'Come on. I want to finish this too.'

'So do I,' said David unconvincingly. Steeling himself, he pushed past Jenny and Jo and began to climb, trying to walk as softly as possible although his hard shoes still made a ringing sound. He paused on the fourth step and listened. The silence seemed to wrap itself round their minds now, deadening their senses.

'Can you see anything?' Jo whispered.

'Not so far. I'll keep going,' said David, not moving.

Jenny stood on the first step with Jo close behind her, looking petrified.

Then a baby began to cry so loudly that David almost fell and Jenny gave a little whimper of fear.

'Why does the baby need me?' Jo was shaking.

'Come on,' said Jenny. 'We'll go and find out.'

David slowly began to climb again and the

others followed. As they did so the creaking broke out and then the clicking, as an accompaniment to the crying of the baby which gradually grew louder as if in competition. Eventually the frenzied din was so intense that each individual noise was barely distinguishable. Despite the raucous clamour David kept climbing, and soon Jo and Jenny were about halfway up the staircase behind him.

The cobwebs were thick, and as he pushed dusty fronds aside several slight scamperings across his hands and face made him realise he was disturbing the haunts of spiders that had not been invaded for years. But the terrible din of the sounds in his head made David push on, hardly noticing the stirrings and scamperings and the light touches that would normally have made him cry out in disgust.

Then, just as suddenly as the sounds had started, the crying of the baby, the frantic creaking and the monotonous clicking came to an abrupt halt.

David gazed into the tangle of cobwebs, letting his beam probe the darkness, one hand on a thick strand, puzzled at what he had seen, not sure where the baleful eyes were coming from.

Then the dusty mass stirred, a taloned claw ripped through and the owl was on him, screeching over his head, jabbing with a scaly beak.

David felt sharp pain on his cheek and then something warm and sticky began to trickle down his face. He clung on to the stair rail, determinedly pulling himself forward. There could be no going back now.

'It's only instinct,' David muttered. Where was the thing now, he wondered.

'Are you all right, Dave?' called Jenny fearfully.

'It was only a graze. Let's keep going.'

He came to another abrupt halt, his beam playing on a gap where at least four more stairs must once have been. Now they had rusted away, and when David swept the vaulted roof of the tower he could see a large hole that must have let in rain for years.

Cobwebs stretched across the space between the last stair and the landing above. David wondered if he could reach through them, find some kind of hand-hold and drag himself up. Suppose the owl attacked again? He could be thrown down on to the stone flags below and the drop was at least ten metres. But he had to take the risk, had to reach the landing.

'There aren't any more steps, but I think I can pull myself up.'

'Don't take any really bad risks,' warned Jenny

anxiously.

Jo said nothing.

Suddenly the baby began to cry. The wailing was plaintive this time, the sound thin and weak.

'Listen,' said David. 'I'm going to get myself on the landing and try and hook my ankles round something. Then I can pull you up, and we can both pull Jo up.'

'It would be better the other way round,' Jenny replied. 'Jo's much lighter than me. I'll go last.'

'OK.' David was disappointed. He was more afraid of the landing than the drop and he had wanted his sister, calm and reliable as she always was, up there with him. Jo was so unpredictable. But he knew that Jenny was right.

He gazed up at the floor above, climbing as high as he dared on the broken stairway, holding the bike lamp as tightly as he could and reaching up, brushing against more layers of cobwebs. His fingers fumbled for a grip but found only soft pulpy wood that came away at his touch.

David swayed, grabbed the top of the stairs, almost lost the bike lamp and steadied himself, gasping a little, the sweat running down his forehead, the panic gnawing away at his resolve.

'OK?' yelled Jenny.

'Sort of.' Why didn't Jo say anything, he wondered angrily. Was she just a passenger? Getting them to do all the hard work so that her mysterious mission could be fulfilled? Then he felt ashamed of himself when he remembered what Jo had been through and how terrified she had been. She was probably just numb.

David played the beam carefully around the floor above, searching for an object he could grab. As he did so, the baby's cries seemed to become weaker.

'He's not going to make it,' whispered Jo.

'He's resourceful. You'll see.'

'I don't mean him,' Jo hissed. 'I mean Peter. I've got to get to him. Can't you tell David to hurry up?'

'No!' Jenny was angry. 'My brother's doing his best and he can't do any more.' She realised that this was the first time Jo had used the baby's name.

'I'm sorry. It's just that crying.'

'I know. It's awful.' Jenny shivered. The cold seemed to bite into her heart. Jo was not only obsessed but also in the power of the Dark Tower.

David swept the landing yet again with his beam. A safety rail had once run round the entire area but sections had either rotted or broken away. Nevertheless parts remained, although he had no idea how stable they might be. They were also almost out of reach. Suppose he *could* make a grab for the rail? If he found a strong section, he could hook his ankles round it and pull Jo up. Together they should be able to get Jenny on to the landing.

David edged forward on to the last step, gripped the hook of the bike lamp between his teeth and stretched up, but his hand didn't even brush the bottom of the rail. Somehow he would have to jump and make a grab for it. If he missed – but David was determined not to think about that, nor the fact that his teeth were hurting badly.

'Don't try it,' said Jenny. 'It's too dodgy.' He knew how afraid she was for him and David didn't want to dwell on that either. He had to take the risk before he lost his nerve.

Without any further hesitation, he pushed himself up into space. For a moment he scrabbled at the rail, his mouth open in a silent scream, the bike lamp falling into the shadowy drop below.

David heard it hit the stone flags. Now he'd managed to grab the rail with one hand, and he swung in space, his arm feeling as if it was being wrenched out of its socket.

In agony now, he dragged himself up again and by some miracle managed to secure a grip with his left hand. But David was still hanging over the drop, and somehow had to get his feet on the landing before his arms were pulled out of their sockets.

Desperately, using every ounce of his strength, he kicked out with his legs, trying to double himself up, to get at least one foot round the rail and edge himself along to where the spiral staircase had originally been. But he didn't have the strength and he knew that the little he had left was draining fast. His arm muscles screamed as the rest of his body weighed him down.

'I'm falling,' he yelled.

'No, you're not. Try again.' Jenny's voice was calm but he detected the raw fear.

Then Jo said quietly, 'Go for it, David. Go for it again. You'll do it this time.'

The baby's cries were soft now and above them David could hear a new sound, rather like the sombre ticking of a grandfather clock.

Energy suddenly surged through his body like electricity, and as he swung his legs up again the ache in his arms disappeared. Almost immediately his feet made contact and then locked around a strut, and he began to inch his way along the underside of the rail until he could slide beneath the rusty, flaking metal and on to the dusty landing. He lay there gasping, the miraculous new energy gone, every muscle in his body leaden, aching and incredibly painful.

'What did you do?' he gasped.

'I don't know what you mean.' Jo's voice echoed up from below.

'You gave me power.'

'It was just confidence.'

'No. It was like a battery charge.' David stumbled to his feet and bumped into the clock. There was a dim glow, and gazing up he saw that another hole in the roof was letting in faint moonlight. Had the dense blanket of fog lifted? Was it getting any clearer outside? Not that that would help in any way. It was Jo who had so miraculously come to his aid.

David looked at the grandfather clock and was just able to see that the hands were shaped like rooks and each figure of the hour was adorned with a crow.

'Come on,' shouted Jenny. 'What are you doing? There's no point in hanging about.'

But David was staring at the clock, and as he did

so the ticking suddenly stopped. Had that been part of his amazing energy too?

David got Jo on to the landing by locking his ankles around the post and leaning out sideways. She came swinging up into his arms, hardly seeming to weigh anything at all, handing him the other bike lamp. Jenny was heavier, but between the two of them they pulled her up without much difficulty.

They all three stood panting on the landing, listening to the soft breathing of the baby that was suddenly broken by a wheezing cough. Slowly the creaking sound began again, but when they gazed down the length of the landing there was only darkness, which even the lamp couldn't penetrate.

Then Jenny saw the dim outline of a rocking chair slowly creaking to and fro. In it sat a hunched figure. Above the creaking they could hear the click of knitting needles.

For a while no one dared to move. Then, as Jo began to step cautiously forward, the rocking chair lost momentum and soon it was almost still.

'Come on,' whispered Jenny. 'We can't leave Jo alone.'

The twins stumbled down the landing towards the rocking chair until they were standing just behind it, seeing gnarled hands gripping its sides. Jo's face was rigid, her eyes glazed. Then the figure began to turn towards them.

David bit his tongue painfully, barely able to contain his horror and revulsion. The figure had an old woman's face that was not quite there. The parchment skin was translucent, showing the bones of the skull below.

'I must go and look after Peter,' said Jo. 'He needs me. She can't help him any longer.' Her voice was matter of fact. Jo began to walk past the chair, but it was almost blocking the landing and Jenny grabbed her arm.

The old lady in the chair smiled a terrible smile. She wore a cap, a long black dress and an apron. As the chair started to rock again, the nurse's features began to dissolve, and the cap and apron silvered into a choking cloud of dust.

Through a shimmering haze, the landing seemed to shift and distort and then to reassemble itself. The walls were now covered with a red-embossed paper, the face of the grandfather clock was restored to a pristine shine, its birds freshly painted. Next to the clock was a table covered with sketches of rooks and crows, and above it hung prints showing birds in flight. Then the haze began to thin and the vision faded into bleak, web-hung devastation.

'Don't let her go,' yelled Jenny to David as Jo slipped out of her grasp. They ran after her, but Jo was hurrying towards a door that was framed by a black mass of dark, shifting feathers.

CHAPTER TWELVE

Slowly the birds rose, hovering in the air, wings beating silently at first and then with a growing clamour. The landing was filled with an acrid smell and the roar of flight. The dark bodies pressed closer, almost like a swarm of monster bees, and then slowly fluttered apart, as if inviting entry.

'No!' yelled David. 'Don't go in, Jo. Stay with us.' Dimly he could hear the baby crying and then it grew louder as the birds rose again and the door slowly opened.

With a cry of delight, Jo ran inside without the slightest sign of fear or anxiety. She looked relaxed and happy. We've failed her, thought Jenny with a sick feeling of despair.

The birds swarmed again, the beating of their wings now more like rattling drums as they dived towards the twins, eyes glowing like tiny coals, talons and beaks poised.

They attacked within seconds, driving David and Jenny back round the landing, the pecking reaching every exposed surface of their bodies until the sharp little pin-pricks became unbearable. They knew they couldn't fight back, knew they stood no chance against the snapping beaks.

As they passed the rocking chair, it began to move again, this time much more rapidly. But the old woman was no longer there.

The birds flew high up to the ceiling of the tower, hovering above David and Jenny. They both knew they had to make a stand, had to get back to Jo, but how could they possibly evade them?

Then Jenny gasped. A snowy white owl had suddenly materialised in the rocking chair, bathed in filtered moonlight, baleful eyes gazing up at the twins as it rocked itself to and fro.

'Don't harm Jo,' whispered David. 'Please don't harm her.'

But the owl simply glared back at them.

David gazed up, seeing the black mass above them waiting to attack again. What was going to happen to Jo? What would they do to her?

Then the birds began to descend, a dark cloud full of snapping beaks, and the chair began to rock faster, the owl watching them triumphantly.

'Come on,' yelled Jenny. 'If we don't move they'll make us fall over those broken stairs.'

But wasn't that the idea? thought David. Wasn't that exactly what the birds planned to do? Kill them?

At the edge of the drop Jenny gasped, 'Can you reach down with your feet?'

'I don't know. I think so if I hang on to the rail.'

'Do it fast. Go first.'

David sat down, grabbed the rail and slid under it, flailing out, kicking air and finding no support.

'Lean out some more,' yelled Jenny. 'You haven't got far to go.'

David grabbed the rail with one hand and felt his foot touch the top step of the spiral staircase. Could he somehow balance himself? Or would he slip and fall on to the stone-flagged floor below? He glanced up at the birds which were hovering lower now, their wings beating dryly, urging him on, suspending their attack, no doubt hoping he would soon plunge down to his death.

'Go for it,' whispered Jenny fearfully.

David knew he had to take the risk and let himself go, but panic filled him and he was sure he would fall. Meanwhile, the birds were slowly and relentlessly descending.

David couldn't see anything below.

'Can you do it?' whispered Jenny.

'I think so.'

'Why don't you give me the lamp?'

'I'll need it for you. Don't worry. I'll be OK.' He pushed the lamp inside the front of his jacket.

The black cloud of birds was just above Jenny's head now, hovering, waiting.

David let go of the rail.

Jenny gave a little whimper of fear as he launched himself into black space and hit the top of the spiral staircase with his feet, swaying and then gripping the rail with both hands.

'Got it!' he yelled, sweat pouring into his eyes. He stood there for a few seconds, gasping for air. Taking the lamp in one hand, he flashed it up at Jenny's terrified face. 'Just lower yourself down and I'll take your legs.'

'OK.' Jenny did as she was told, grabbing the rail and then dropping, trusting David completely. He clutched at her knees, pulling his twin towards him so they both stood crushed together on the top step.

'You OK?' said David, squeezing past her and starting to climb down.

'I'm fine.' But she wasn't. Now the worst was

over she was shaking and sweating and trembling so much that she could hardly put one foot in front of the other.

Gradually, trying to calm herself, Jenny followed David down the spiral staircase, conscious that the birds must still be hovering, waiting and watching. They were driving them out of the Dark Tower, keeping Jo prisoner.

Once the twins were back on the stone-flagged floor they stood gazing up into the darkness, knowing they had been outmanoeuvred and out-witted.

'We can't leave her,' said David.

'But what are we going to do?'

'We'd better talk outside.'

'I'm sure they can't hear us,' said Jenny, but she reduced her voice to a whisper. 'All they have is instinct. They won't be able to understand what we're saying.'

'I wouldn't like to bet on that,' said David.

Then one of the rooks dive-bombed them, snapping with its beak and raking with its claws.

'Suicide mission,' yelled David, hitting out with one fist and holding the lamp with the other.

But the rook simply landed on Jenny's head and jabbed with its beak. With a scream of pain she ran, the bird still in her hair, feeling for the door which she eventually found, but although she tugged fiercely it refused to yield.

David ran towards his sister, beating at the rook which still clung to her hair with its claws.

'Help me get the door open,' she shouted. 'Forget the bird!'

Together they pulled at the handle, but it still showed no sign of opening. Then the door suddenly gave, so abruptly that David and Jenny were thrown on to the floor, and the rook flew up, making a raucous cawing sound which was immediately taken up by the other birds.

'Go for it!' yelled David.

The twins picked themselves up and ran out into the freezing fog as the cawing reached new heights of triumph and the door of the Dark Tower slammed behind them.

CHAPTER THIRTEEN

David and Jenny stood gasping for air, not noticing the bitter cold or the dense fog that seeped into their lungs, making them cough. Fairfax Park could hardly be seen, only the occasional treetop breaking through the dense grey blanket. They both felt a total sense of failure.

'We *can't* leave her,' said Jenny.

'I'll call the police – or the fire brigade. They'll get her out.' David was desperate.

'If they try, I've got this feeling the birds will turn on her. Peck Jo to death.'

'But why?' David was bewildered. 'She's there for a purpose.'

'Yes, but I'm sure if anyone interferes with that purpose they'll kill her.' Jenny sounded convincing. Then she hissed, 'What's that?'

They could both hear someone walking hesitantly through the gates of Fairfax Park.

Jenny and David hid behind one of the oaks, but as the fog was thick they had no real need to conceal themselves.

Uncertain footsteps stumbled towards them and then a voice, indistinct and agitated, came out of the blanket.

'Is anyone there? Jo? Are you there, Jo?'

It was Bob Grant.

David called back at once. 'We're over here. It's David and Jenny Golding.'

'Where?'

'Follow my voice.'

Slowly, rather like a wraith himself, Mr Grant came into sight. 'Where's Jo?'

'In the Dark Tower.'

Jenny quickly began to explain.

When she had finished, Bob Grant shook his head in confusion and the twins had no idea whether he had believed them or not. 'I should have told her.'

'Told her what?' asked David uncertainly.

'The strange story that's been in the family for generations, but because she was so nervy I never bothered her with it.' He gazed at them suspiciously. 'You wouldn't be playing some stupid game, would you?' he said, and David couldn't bear the painful hope in his eyes. He turned away, gazing at the door of the tower, suddenly revealed as the fog parted slightly.

Jenny was indignant. 'All you have to do is look at the cuts on our faces. They were made by beaks, Mr Grant, and they're painful.'

'I'm sorry.' He was immediately penitent and the twins could both see that Jo's father was almost at breaking point. 'But these birds – what are they doing?'

'They're driven by some kind of instinct,' said David.

'The story says that Sir James was buried in an unconsecrated grave – unconsecrated because he committed suicide,' said Bob Grant reluctantly. 'His spirit's always been reputed to be trapped in the tower and it can only be released if he's buried in the family tomb at St Lawrence's. Of course, it's only a—'

'We forgot to tell you,' Jenny broke in. 'We found the grave. It's round the back of the tower.' Then she paused and corrected herself. 'At least – Jo found it.'

Mr Grant still looked confused, as if doubt and belief were locked in battle inside him and he didn't know which of them to pick.

'Why have the birds chosen Jo?' demanded David.

Bob Grant frowned, trying to find a grain of sense in all this speculation, and failing.

'What I don't understand is – how can you have Sir James as an ancestor when all the family died of typhoid.' Jenny had only just seen the problem but David looked at her impatiently. This wasn't the time to be logical.

'There was an older daughter by his first marriage,' Bob Grant replied brusquely. 'She didn't live at the Hall so she wasn't infected. That's how our line of the family began.'

Jenny nodded, but David could hardly contain himself. Time was rushing past and they were just talking. They should be thinking up a rescue plan. Anything could be happening to Jo up there in the tower.

'Sir James will have to be dug up and reburied in a churchyard,' David said impatiently. 'Then his spirit will be released.' But his mind was full of questions, as was Jenny's. Why had the birds forced Jo into the tower? Could there be something they wanted her to witness?

'It's as if the birds have got something to tell Jo,' said Jenny slowly. 'What could it be?'

'I'm not going to accept any more of this rubbish,' snapped Bob Grant. 'I can't think why I let you sidetrack me like this. All I know is that my daughter's in that tower — or so you say — and I'm going to break down that door and get her out.'

Jenny turned to David. 'Of course — Jo must be psychic, like us. *That's* why the birds wanted her. Even now they could be revealing—'

Bob Grant finally lost his temper. 'I should never have let my daughter anywhere near you two. You've got her into this, haven't you? Jo's highly strung and—'

'She's more than that,' retorted David.

'You keep out of this!' he yelled. 'You shouldn't have interfered in the first place.' He paused and then said more quietly, 'Birds. Spirits. Psychics. It's a load of rubbish. You've driven my Jo out of her mind.'

'We've got experience of this kind of thing,' David protested indignantly.

But Jenny knew that he would only work Jo's father up even more and she quickly intervened. 'Look,' she said. 'I've got this strong feeling the birds need Jo for a purpose. You've *got* to try and take this seriously.'

'Rubbish. I'm not continuing with this ridiculous conversation.'

'Please—'

'You've indoctrinated her.'

Jenny's patience snapped too. 'We *haven't* indoctrinated her!'

'I'm going to the police,' yelled Bob Grant. 'And you're going to be in real trouble.'

How can *they* help, thought David, now equally angry. Your daughter's in the Dark Tower with a flock of birds and a ghostly baby. You could get her killed.

Jenny, however, had regained control. 'I've got a plan that might work.'

'And what might that be?' Bob Grant asked with evident scepticism.

'St Lawrence's church isn't far from here, is it? Suppose David and I went to the graveyard and found the Fairfax family tomb?'

'What good would that do?' He was openly scoffing at them now.

'We found some words scratched on the unconsecrated grave and we think there might be more clues on the tomb.'

'I'm going to the police.' Bob Grant was calmer now but even more resolute. 'You have to realise you are both dangerously deluded. I'm holding you personally responsible for playing on my daughter's imagination.' He gazed up at the fragments of the tower that could occasionally be seen through the fog. 'Now is she up there or not?'

David and Jenny exchanged an anxious glance. Mr Grant was becoming a major stumbling block. Valuable time was being lost and if he *did* call the police they were both sure Jo was going to be in even greater danger.

'I'm going to the nearest phone box. That's *got* to be the right decision.'

'It's not,' said David bleakly. 'It's really not.'

'Wait a minute,' Jenny intervened again. 'Isn't that Jo's voice?'

For a moment all they could hear was a rhythmic murmur accompanied by the slow flapping of wings, but gradually the song became louder and Bob Grant's expression changed from anger to amazement and then to a kind of awful despair.

Jo was singing a lullaby, her voice low and sweet and clear.

> 'Rock-a-bye, baby,
> Thy cradle is green,
> Father's a nobleman,
> Mother's a queen.'

Mr Grant began to run towards the Dark Tower and Jenny and David followed, losing him for a moment in the fog. When they caught up with him he was standing at its foot, shouting up at the top window. 'Jo. It's Dad. Come down now! I love you. I love you, Jo—'

His pleading was heart-rending, but it didn't make the slightest difference. Jo continued to sing as if she'd heard nothing. The ivy rustled menacingly, although the fog was as thick as ever and there was not the slightest suggestion of a breath of wind.

'And Betty's a lady,
And wears a gold ring;
And Johnny's a drummer,
And drums for the King.'

'Jo!' yelled Bob Grant. 'Come to the window, Jo. Please come.'

'It's no good,' said Jenny, gently taking him by the arm.

But he shook her off impatiently, just as Jo started a new song.

'Baa, baa, black sheep
Have you any wool?
Yes, sir, yes, sir,
Three bags full.'

'It's Dad, Jo,' Bob Grant yelled again. 'It's your dad. I love you, Jo. I love you so much.'

'One for the master,
And one for the dame,
And one for the little boy
Who lives down the lane.'

'Jo!' Her father was getting hoarse now. 'Please, Jo!'

The song ended and they could all hear the faint gurgling of a baby. Then the wheezing began, gathering in strength until it seemed as if the Dark Tower itself was fighting for breath.

'Watch out,' yelled David as the crow suddenly hurtled out of the fog, slashing at Bob Grant's cheek with its beak and then vanishing into the murk again. He fell back, clapping his hand to his face, and David and Jenny saw the bright red blood slide between his fingers and down his chin.

'*Now* do you believe us?' yelled David.

He didn't reply. Then Bob Grant said quietly, his lips trembling, 'I'll stay here while you go to St Lawrence's. I can tell you where the family tomb is, although I don't see how it can help us, do you?' He looked at them both in sudden hope.

'It might,' replied David. 'Anyway, we've got to try something.'

When Mr Grant had finished giving them directions, Jenny said, 'We'd be really grateful if you could ring our parents and say we're still helping Jo and we're safe.'

'You want me to lie to them?'

'If you want us to help you get Jo out of the tower, you've got to help *us*.'

Suddenly Bob Grant broke down and he turned to Jenny pleadingly. 'You've got to help Jo. I want her out of there.' Then, without warning, he ran to the door of the Dark Tower and tried to open it. But it wouldn't move. 'I'll break it down!' he screamed, and threw himself at the battered, paint-scarred wood. Directly he made contact, however, Bob Grant was hurled backwards on to the ground. As he lay on the frosty grass, bruised and winded, all they could hear was the cawing of a rook from somewhere behind the door.

'Please,' said David. 'Ring our parents.' He paused. 'We *can* help you know.'

Bob Grant still looked far from convinced.

Jenny and David ran towards the gates of Fairfax Park, grabbed their bikes and sped off down the road to St Lawrence's. Jenny had no lamp, but she knew she had to keep going somehow. It was only a short while before they heard the beating of wings high up in the fog and knew they were under surveillance.

CHAPTER FOURTEEN

The large churchyard was neglected and over-grown, and although Jo's father's directions had been precise they were hard to follow in the fog.

Knowing that time was running out, Jenny and David pushed their way through the damp, waist-high grass, trying to avoid the crosses and mauso-leums, plaques and tombs, all of whose inscriptions were faded and covered in dank moss.

'The Fairfax family tomb is down at the end, facing south. It looks like a miniature chapel, with columns,' Bob Grant had told them, but the twins were still a long time searching.

It was Jenny who finally spotted it, half buried in brambles and with a yew tree leaning against one of the columns, cracking it from end to end.

The bike lamp still had a powerful beam, but it was difficult to read the faded lettering. Then, just when they were both about to give up in frustration, David found the inscription they both wanted.

IN LOVING MEMORY OF
LADY ALICE CONSTANCE ANNABELLA FAIRFAX
WHO WAS TRAGICALLY TAKEN BY TYPHOID
ON THE NIGHT OF MARCH 14TH, 1886,
AGED 29 YEARS
ALSO IN LOVING MEMORY OF HER BELOVED SON
PETER JAMES ARTHUR FAIRFAX
WHO WASTED AWAY FROM THE SAME DISEASE
ON MARCH 22ND, 1886, AGED SEVEN MONTHS

'Wait a minute,' said Jenny. 'There's something else underneath all this moss.'

As she scratched away at the stone a crudely carved rook's head was revealed and then a crow's.

'What's that meant to mean?' gasped David, the fear turning his stomach to ice.

Jenny worked away, her fingers numb with the cold.

'Let's have a go.'

'No. I'm almost there.' She was scrabbling even more furiously than before.

A few minutes later Jenny discovered an even more crudely carved inscription, as if an amateur had hacked at the surface under the cover of darkness. The lettering was uneven and hard to make out but they finally read:

SIR JAMES FAIRFAX,
FATHER OF THE LIGHT AND HOPE OF MY LIFE
I MUST RIGHT THIS WRONG OR NEVER REST.

A.W.

'Someone added that. It's just scratched on,' said Jenny. 'Could it have been the nurse?'

Meanwhile, David was checking for more names and halfway up the other side of the tomb found one that didn't belong to the family.

ANNA PATIENCE WOLFF
FAITHFUL SERVANT TO THE FAIRFAX FAMILY
WHO SUPPORTED THEM IN THEIR DARKEST HOUR
DIED APRIL 2ND, 1898, AGED 75 YEARS
RIP

'It looks as if she died of old age – not typhoid. Do you think the Church will allow Sir James to be buried here?' he said doubtfully. 'That *must* be what the birds and Anna Wolff want. This scratched inscription just isn't enough after all he did for them. But what guarantee can we give them? The vicar might refuse. It might cost too much money.'

But Jenny was thinking aloud, 'Anna Wolff. She

obviously loved Peter. Maybe she loved him too much.'

'What do you mean?' demanded David.

'I'm not sure. It's just a feeling I've got.' She hurriedly changed the subject. 'We could do some fund-raising,' she suggested. 'For the reburial, I mean.'

'Digging up Sir James from one grave and putting him in another is a bit different from the school swimming-pool appeal.'

'It could be a local community project.' She was determined not to be disheartened.

'Why should anyone care?' David was equally determined to be realistic.

'They've got to be *made* to care.' But Jenny sounded vague, as if she was still thinking about something else.

The twins cycled back through the fog as fast as they dared with only one lamp, sometimes hearing the beating of wings above them. Jenny kept seeing her mother's face in the kitchen, trying to be brave and generous at the same time. Had Jo's father managed to reassure her, or had he just rung the police? There was no telling what he would do, thought David miserably.

Reaching the park, they concealed their bikes in the shrubs again, and ran through the half-open gates. It seemed even colder now, and although the ride had set their pulses racing, David and Jenny felt frozen as they hurried across to the Dark Tower only to find it silent and deserted. There was no sign of any birds. Worse still there was no sign of Mr Grant.

Then he stepped out of the shadows, making both Jenny and David's hearts give a sickening lurch.

'She's been silent,' he gabbled. 'Totally silent since you left. I spoke to your mother and she asked a lot of questions. I told her Jo had been bullied again and you were helping her. I didn't say the bullies might be a flock of birds.' He paused for breath. 'Your mother sounds a good woman. I'd like to thank her if we ever get Jo out of the tower. I hated lying to her. What if—'

The singing suddenly began again, as if recognising the twins' return. Jo's voice was serene, as if she was already a part of the memory vault of the Dark Tower.

'You shall have an apple,
You shall have a plum,
You shall have a rattle-basket
When your daddy comes home.'

The song ended on a soft clear note and then Jo began another.

'A wise old owl sat in an oak,
The more he heard the less he spoke;
The less he spoke the more he heard.
Why aren't we all like that wise old bird?'

'I can't stand any more of this,' whispered Bob Grant.

Neither could the twins, and Jenny ran to the rustling ivy and began to climb. David followed her without hesitating.

Despite its unpleasant silkiness, the ivy was strong and the climb easy. Taking different routes through the tendrils, the twins soon arrived at the top window and peered inside.

Candles had been placed on an old box near the door and flickering flames threw shadows on to the cobwebbed walls. A cradle was in the centre of the floor and the rooks and crows were crouched as if they were nesting. The snowy owl was rocking the cradle to and fro, whilst Jo gazed down at the bloated and feverish face of the baby. Peter only gave out little wheezing sounds. He no longer had the strength to cry.

In contrast to the bitter cold outside, the room radiated heat as if it was transmitting fever.

David said Jo's name gently, afraid of breaking the spell. Immediately the eyes of the birds turned threateningly towards him, but Jo didn't even look round or appear to hear.

There was a shuffling movement from the floor, but the rooks and crows remained where they were, although the twins could sense mounting hostility.

Then, slowly, Jo turned towards David and Jenny as if realising their presence for the first time. But she didn't seem to recognise them and her eyes were blank.

'You have to trust us.' David didn't sound very confident, and gazed anxiously from Jo to the baby to the roosting birds.

'Come in,' said Jo.

David hesitated. How could they go into that plague-ridden hothouse? The birds were bound to attack them as soon as they put a foot on the sill. 'Can we trust *you*?' he asked her.

But Jo didn't reply and they could now hear the sound of the rocking chair from the corridor outside the circular room. Then the knitting needles began to click.

CHAPTER FIFTEEN

David made up his mind. 'We're not coming in,' he said firmly.

'You said we have to trust you,' said Jo. 'Now you have to trust us.'

'She's right,' Jenny snapped at her brother. 'We've all got to trust one another.'

But David still hesitated, gazing down at Mr Grant hovering anxiously in the fog. 'Your father's outside,' he said, desperately trying to reach her.

'I know.' Jo's voice was a monotone again.

'You should reassure him. Say you're all right.'

'Not yet.'

'When *will* you speak to him?'

'When all this is over.'

'Let's go,' said Jenny, pulling herself up the ivy, but David still hung back.

'It's going to be all right,' he called down, forcing himself to convey a confidence he didn't feel. 'Jo's safe and we're going in.'

The rook came out of the fog without warning, soaring through the window, brushing Jenny's hair with its wings. Then the creaking of the rocking chair and the click of the needles became much louder, filling the overheated room with their threatening sound.

Jenny scrambled over the sill and jumped down with David close behind her.

The rook hopped slowly towards them, gazing up with bright, inquisitive eyes as they passed Jo and the owl, catching another glimpse of the suffering baby. The skin on Peter's face was stretched tight, his cheeks red with fever and his eyes dilated. His mouth was open, the wheezing horrible to hear, and there was dried saliva at the corners of his lips.

David tried not to glance at the birds, but he was acutely aware of their brooding shapes and their acrid smell pervaded the room.

The door was ajar, and as if drawn by a magnet David and Jenny walked slowly into the corridor which was dark and lit only by a strange glow. The figure in the chair was hunched and the rocking had slowed, but the clicking of the needles was as fast as ever.

'Anna,' said Jenny quietly. 'Anna Wolff.'

The nurse looked up, her skin like parchment, her bony fingers knitting a baby's cardigan from the ball of wool on her lap. She wore a bonnet and was swathed in blankets.

'We've seen the inscription. You must have loved Peter very much.' Jenny forced out the words.

The eyes in the spectral face glowed and David suddenly felt their power. Anna stared at them intently and then she leant forward, dropping the needles and the half-made cardigan on to the corridor floor. They made no sound. At the same time the chair stopped rocking and Jenny and David could see frost beginning to form on the walls of the Dark Tower.

Slowly Anna Wolff's wraith rose and beckoned to them, and as they nervously edged nearer she began to drift towards one of the round windows.

When they moved in her direction, the twins felt icy cold and suddenly terribly angry. They heard the wheezing of the baby and the nurse's voice entered their minds painfully, making their heads throb.

Peter, my dearest. Oh, Peter, you have to go on living for Anna. I love you so dearly, my sweetheart. Live for me. Not for that selfish wretch of a father of yours. Live for me. Live for me. Live for me.

The words repeated themselves like hammer blows to David and Jenny's hearts and they both realised how much Anna Wolff had hated Sir James for infecting her helpless charge with his typhoid while, ironically, the carrier made a good recovery himself.

Then Anna's voice in their minds became even more insistent, even more full of hatred.

You're killing him, sir. If my Peter dies, I'll hold you responsible.

It's her, thought David. It's Anna who's the source of the Dark Tower's power. Not the birds after all. They're still trying to protect Sir James, to save him from the consequences of what happened, but Anna has side-tracked Jo into caring for the dying baby.

There was no fog. Smooth lawns led down to where the sad little pond in the neglected park had been. But now it was much larger, with a sparkling fountain that played in the centre and fish swimming in the clear, clean water. The Fairfax garden was in bloom. It was spring.

Soon the birds began to gather on the grass

below. A few at first and then more – rooks and crows and an owl, incongruous in the spring sun, looking vulnerable.

A cry came from further down the corridor and David and Jenny turned to see a tall figure with long dark hair. His face was twisted with grief and tears were running down his hollow cheeks. He was shouting something but the sound was distorted. Then, as he ran towards the nursery, David and Jenny could see more clearly Sir James Fairfax's appalling grief. They ducked but he went through them with a rush of cold air, disappearing into the nursery. Then there was a desolate cry and he repeated his dead son's name over and over again.

But that was nothing to the cry of rage that followed from Anna Wolff.

Sir James emerged again from the nursery, backing down the landing, his arms thrown forward protectively as the devoted nurse, the knitting needle held high, began to advance on him, step by step, her eyes blazing that awesome power.

Sir James continued to back away from her as she screamed in the twins' minds, *You killed him. You killed my baby.*

Anna Wolff began to run at him now and he fled, heading for the stairs. At the last minute he turned, determined to calm her, but before he could speak she lunged at him fiercely. Somehow Sir James dodged her, but now he was beyond the stairs and had his back against the large round window.

You killed my baby. Her pain and rage seared David and Jenny. Then as Anna slashed out at Sir James with the knitting needle yet again they saw him fall against the glass. It smashed in slow motion, shards splintering. For a moment he seemed to hang there and then toppled backwards, his features twisted with guilt and grief and fear. As he tumbled over and over towards the ground, the birds rose up, fluttering, cawing, a black cloud but not dense enough to catch him as he fell through them to the path below. He lay very still and Anna Wolff peered out through the broken glass, her wraith gradually dissolving into nothing at all. In the twins' minds one word lingered: *murderer.*

Silently Jo joined David and Jenny at the round window, but as they gazed down the scene changed. It was late afternoon and a group of men were carrying a cheap and plain-looking coffin round the back of the tower. There were no mourners. No priest. Only Anna Wolff, dressed in a black coat and scarf, walking slowly behind the coffin. Above her, the rooks and crows hovered threateningly.

Then a rook plunged towards her, its beak lacerating her cheek. At the same time a crow dived towards her bonnet. The men put down the coffin and began to beat at the dark feathers as they covered Anna Wolff. Eventually they succeeded in dislodging the birds, killing some and scattering the majority.

Slowly Anna got to her feet, her face streaming blood. Declining assistance, she struggled away, stepping over the corpses of the crows and rooks.

Shrugging, the men picked up the coffin again and began to carry it round to the back of the Dark Tower.

As Anna slowly walked away, the flock of birds swooped low over her head. Soon she was lost to sight and the garden darkened slightly, as if in twilight.

'The family never realised she killed Sir James,' whispered David. 'Only the birds knew.'

'No wonder she never left her cottage,' said Jenny. 'The birds would have been waiting for her.'

'She was a good and faithful servant, she just loved Peter too much,' said Jo.

'No,' said David sharply. 'Anna was possessive. She was obsessed with her love for the baby, for Peter. Sir James wasn't a murderer. He couldn't help being a typhoid carrier. It was Anna Wolff who was the killer. In the end we were too strong for her. She had to show us the truth.'

'Yes, but she was obviously racked with guilt during her life. That's why she wrote those inscriptions. She needed to unburden herself,' said Jenny.

Jo didn't seem to be listening. She was already walking back down the long dark corridor.

'The birds brought her.' David sounded confident. 'They needed to explain.'

As he spoke, the twins heard the ticking of the grandfather clock and they hurried back down the landing.

Jo had closed the door behind her and the corridor was dark, yet as the twins approached the clock its face seemed to have a slight glow and they could make out the birds. As David and Jenny watched, the hands began to turn and the tower was filled with the sound of a rocking chair creaking, needles clicking, birds cawing, a baby crying and Sir James's voice screaming Peter's name.

The grandfather clock chimed the hour every

few seconds and the creaking and the clicking, the crying, the cawing and the screaming began all over again, rising in such volume that Jenny and David thought their eardrums would burst.

'Stop!' yelled David. 'It's all right. We know. We understand.'

Suddenly the dreadful noise came to an abrupt halt, but the silence seemed just as loud.

'Tell the birds to release Jo,' yelled David and then saw that the door had opened and a rook was watching them from the doorway, eventually hopping back into the circular room. Then the owl appeared, flying towards the rocking chair. The dust flew up, hazing around the twins, and the chair began to rock again, and as David stepped out of the way he trod on something that rolled and clattered. He bent down and picked up the knitting needles which still held a scrap of wool.

There was a fluttering sound and they saw the birds flying out of the room and down the corridor towards them, soaring above them in a rush of feathers and then out of the window into the foggy night. The owl, however, remained perched on the rocking chair, watching them intently.

Slowly David and Jenny continued to walk down the corridor. When they reached the circular room they could see that Jo was kneeling beside a bundle of rags and the wooden poles that had once been Peter's cradle.

'It's over,' said Jenny, putting her arms round Jo.

Jo was confused and afraid. 'Will the birds come back?' she asked warily. 'Will they want me again?'

'No,' said David confidently. 'Never.'

Epilogue

David and Jenny and their parents stood with Jo and her father at the base of the Dark Tower on a sunny Sunday afternoon in April. They were watching Sir James's coffin being carried with dignity by the staff of a local undertakers into the back of a hearse.

Bob Grant had been so grateful for the rescue of his daughter from the Dark Tower that he had run a one-man campaign to get Sir James Fairfax's body exhumed and reburied in the family tomb in St Lawrence's churchyard. The real explanation, however, had not been revealed because, as the twins knew, it would never have been believed. The reason for the burial of Sir James Fairfax's remains in the family tomb was only seen as a merciful act.

The money had been raised by a charity, the

vicar had been co-operative and Sir James's name had been cut into the family tomb by a local stonemason.

During the months that had passed while the arrangements were being made, neither the twins nor Jo had been visited by the birds. Clearly they had been trusted. Bob Grant, however, had still not come to terms with what had really happened in the Dark Tower and had told everyone, including the press, that Jo had wandered into the building and had somehow managed to get trapped in an upstairs room, later to be rescued by David and Jenny.

It seemed to all three of them that this was the best explanation, particularly as Jo had almost forgotten what had happened to her, only retaining a phobia about birds. She was much more relaxed, both at home and at school, making friends and doing better with her work.

'I'm really proud of you two,' said Mr Golding as the undertakers closed the rear door of the hearse. 'You've been a real friend to Jo.'

'I still can't believe you climbed up that ivy,' said Mrs Golding, gazing at the Dark Tower in dismay. 'It must have been terribly dangerous.'

Obviously feeling they had been negligent, the

Council had sealed the entrance to the tower and covered the windows with steel sheeting. Now even the birds couldn't get in.

But, in fact, they seemed to have lost interest. The rookery was deserted and the crows were nesting elsewhere.

As the hearse began to drive away, Bob Grant said, 'That's a real coincidence, isn't it?'

A solitary rook and an equally solitary crow were hovering over the hearse, as if saying farewell to Sir James Fairfax. Then David heard a familiar sound from the tower. The muffled chiming of a grand-father clock. He glanced at Jenny who nodded.

'The Dark Tower's taking leave of Sir James,' she whispered.

'What are you two talking about?' demanded Jo.

'Can't you hear the clock?' asked David.

'What clock? I can't hear anything,' exclaimed Mr Grant, frowning.

Then the chiming stopped and the tower was silent and desolate.

David and Jenny watched the hearse disappear round the corner. After a while, all they could hear was a very faint cawing.